SUPPRESSION

LAUREL SPRINGS EMERGENCY RESPONSE TEAM #2

LARAMIE BRISCOE

Editor: Elfwerks Editing

Beta Readers: Keyla Handley, Danielle Wentworth

Proofreader: Danielle Wentworth

Cover: Laramie Briscoe

Cover Photography: Wander Aguiar

Formatting: Laramie Briscoe

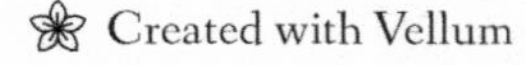

Created with Vellum

ALSO BY LARAMIE BRISCOE

Heaven Hill Series

Meant To Be

Out of Darkness

Losing Control

Worth The Battle

Dirty Little Secret

Second Chance Love

Rough Patch

Beginning of Forever

Home Free

Shield My Heart

A Heaven Hill Christmas

Heaven Hill Next Generation

Hurricane

Wild

Rockin' Country Series

Only The Beginning

One Day at A Time

The Price of Love

Full Circle

Hard To Love

Reaper's Girl

The Moonshine Task Force Series

Renegade

Tank

Havoc

Ace

Menace

Cruise

Stand Alones

Sketch

Sass

Trick

To all the readers, bloggers, and friends who support me every day...thank you!

BLURB

If you don't love, you can't get hurt…

Nick Kepler

One thing my childhood taught me was never show my emotions. Don't make memories. Don't count on other people. Don't hope for the best.

All that changed when I was adopted by Ryan and Whitney Kepler.

Begrudgingly I let them into my life, along with my new sister and a best friend I would lay down my life for. But giving up my heart and accepting love in return from Kelsea Harrison? It's the hardest thing I've ever tried to do.

And the truth is? I'm not sure if I'm that strong.

Kelsea Harrison

From the very moment I met Nick Kepler I knew he would

be the love of my life. Problem is I haven't been able to convince him of that yet.

When our best friends get married, Nick and I spend a drunken night letting our walls down and losing all our inhibitions. In one moment I'm given everything I ever wanted. Then, in the blink of an eye it's taken away from me.

The question is, can I be strong for the both of us?

The answer? I have to be.

ONE

Kelsea

The last thing anyone wants on their wedding day is to puke in the bridal suite. I have it on great authority no one likes to puke, especially right before they put on their wedding dress. Checking out my best friend, Stella? Looks like she didn't get the memo.

"Do we need to get you back to the bathroom?" I whisper as I watch a hand go to her stomach and her other over her mouth. It's almost as if I can literally see her getting greener as the seconds tick by.

"Stella." Whitney's voice carries a tone of disapproval as she turns to face both me and her daughter. "Did you really think it was a good idea to have a wine night with Kels the actual night before your wedding?"

If only Whitney Kepler knew what was actually happening at our wine night. We'd watched *Steel Magnolias*, *Top Gun* and *Sweet Home Alabama* while polishing off a container of cake frosting and giggling about the *something blue* surprise Stella has up her skirt for her groom. Ending up sleeping head-to-head on the couch as we talked about how her brother, Nick, will never get his head out of his ass where I'm concerned. We obviously got very wild.

"Mom, please, not right now." Stella pushes past the both of us, heading for the empty bathroom.

Whitney glares at me as we listen to Stella heave and wretch. It's awful and even I'm having a hard time keeping my gag reflex from acting up. Escaping Whitney's look, I move over to the door, listening closely.

I give her a few moments before I quietly knock on the door. "You okay?"

"C'mon in." Her voice sounds wrecked, and when I open the door, she's sitting on the floor trying to regulate her breathing, her face red and her eyes pooling with tears. She looks to be on this side of panicking and it's my job to get her under control. "You've got to get me some Zofran or I'm not getting through this."

Quickly, I run a rag under the faucet, handing it to her. Meanwhile in my head I'm chanting *you got this* hoping like hell I really do. "You're right. You've got to get your hair and makeup done. Why couldn't you have waited just a few more weeks to get pregnant?"

She snorts, grunting as she lifts herself out of the floor. "Oh sure, you know this wasn't exactly planned. Had we planned it, it would have been about a year from now. How was I supposed to know my birth control would fail big time the one weekend Ransom and I got alone before this wedding?"

My side-eye game is strong as I watch her wipe her face. "Don't even act like the two of you did anything other than fuck like rabbits. I'm sure it had a better chance of failing than actually working."

The smirk she wears is proof enough, and damn if I'm not a

tiny bit jealous. "I'm not apologizing for how hot my soon-to-husband is, and I don't need your judgment. I just need you to find me some Zofran and a can of Sprite."

"Alright." I laugh, not able to deny her anything. There's a reason we've been best friends since we knew what friends actually were. "Let me dodge Whitney. She's pissed because she seriously thinks you and I tied one on last night, but you're the one with the hangover."

"I know, I almost told her, but I truly want this day to be about me and Ransom. When we get back from our honeymoon, we'll tell everybody, I promise. Then you and Nick won't have to keep our secret anymore."

"It's kind of nice keeping a secret with him." I shrug, hoping the tone of my voice doesn't give away how much I enjoy sharing something that's just ours.

Stella's eyes are soft when she looks at me, showing a compassion only she can. "One day it'll be your time, Kels. I promise."

With everything I have, I want to believe her. I'm just not sure I can. How long do I keep waiting? For how many years do I not allow myself to meet new people because I'm afraid once I do, Nicholas Kepler will get his head out of his ass? Instead of acknowledging what she's said to me I paste on an overly enthusiastic smile before I turn from her and square my shoulders as if I'm going to war. "Let me go get you that Zofran and some Sprite. Be back in just a sec."

IT'S a short walk to where the male contingency of this wedding is meeting, but I feel eyes on me from every direction as I go. I've never quite been comfortable with a crowd focusing on me, but I know I make a scene, already wearing my bridesmaid dress. Gathering my courage, I knock on the door to the room where all the men are. "Hey, are y'all decent?"

It opens slowly and I'm greeted on the other side by the dark eyes of the man we were speaking about earlier. "You okay?" There's a tinge of worry in his eyes. "Ransom is freaking the fuck out, afraid that Stella's gonna leave him at the altar. You aren't here to deliver bad news, are you?"

I love Ransom so I don't laugh, but I can't believe he's actually having thoughts that Stella will leave him at the altar. "Is he serious right now?"

Nick laughs and it changes his entire face. I love when he laughs. When he smiles, when he stops taking things so seriously. He turns from someone who looks like he could stomp a hole in the ground to someone who would hold you at night if you asked him to. Maybe I'm the only one who recognizes just how his face changes, but honestly that's okay with me. "He's pussying out hardcore."

"No, I'm not." I hear a disgruntled voice from behind him, watching as Ransom walks toward me. "Is everything okay on your side of things?" If I'm not mistaken, he is looking a little worried.

Turning my attention to Cutter, who became a full-fledged EMT a little over a year ago, I nod. "Yeah, a couple of us, including the bride drank a little too much last night. We need some Zofran, if you can get us some?" We're having photos taken with the first response vehicles because of everyone in the wedding party, so I know an ambulance is around. Since there's only four people at this wedding who know Stella's knocked up, I have to pretend like I'm one of the people nursing a hangover. Running a hand over my forehead for effect, I turn puppy dog eyes up to Cutter.

"There's probably some on the ambulance, and I could

probably scrounge up a bag of fluid, but you and Stella will have to argue over who gets that. Best cure for a hangover."

What a fucking great idea for someone who's been puking off and on all morning. "Ya know what? It's her day, I'll let her have it. Just bring it to me and I'll get her going? It's okay if I look horrible in the pictures, but not her."

"Give me a few minutes." He runs out, buttoning his tux jacket, ready to help.

As I'm leaving, Ransom stops me, grabbing my wrist slightly. His face and eyes show his worry. "Is she really okay?"

"She's pregnant," I deadpan. "She's just got morning sickness, but if we can't settle her stomach, people are gonna find out and this wedding might not happen. Four trips so far, and mama Whit is gettin' suspicious. You know once she brings it up to Ryan this will turn into a whole ordeal. Let me handle this." I reach out and start fixing his collar and tie, smoothing it over. This man, who has always been like a brother to me, I want him to know the woman he loves will be taken care of. "I know it's killing you not to be the one to be helping her right now, Ransom. Trust me, she's in good hands, I promise."

"I know she is, but if you need something, please let me know."

The sincerity in his voice is enough to bring tears to my eyes. These two are going to make such amazing parents, and I know their life together will be blessed with so much happiness.

"Got it." I hear Cutter's voice, turning so I can see him holding up not only a bag of fluid, but a bottle of pills. "Should be good as new in a few minutes. Whatever you don't use, bring back – they do inventory the ambulances. I can explain a few away, but not the whole bottle." He reaches down, hugging me tightly. "In case no one told you today, you're looking hot Harrison."

I roll my eyes, but I can't stop the smile that spreads across my face. Leave it to Cutter to make me blush, even when I don't take half of what he says as truth.

"Thanks!" I grab his loot, ready to get out of dodge before I ruin my makeup. "We'll see you all for pictures. Don't anybody let him run off." I nod to Ransom, grinning before I give the rest of them what I hope is a menacing look.

"They'd have to drag me out."

And that right there is exactly what I want. A man who loves me like he loves Stella, like my dad loves my mom, like my brother loves Ruby. Brushing away the melancholy is hard on a day like today, but I do it as I re-enter the bridal suite. Stella takes a look at what I'm carrying, her head immediately going back with a large shout of approval.

"Oh my God, I love you!" She wraps her arms around me, hugging tightly.

"Come on in here." I point to the bedroom attached, closing the door as we get down to business. "Let's get you fixed up."

After getting her hooked to the IV and getting the pill down, she's getting some color back, and I'm starting to feel better about this whole situation. She doesn't look like she's on death's doorstep, and now I won't have to watch Whit give us both the death glare. At my age it should feel easier to shoulder disappointment from an elder, but it's not. Maybe that's why I'm feeling weird for knowing Stelle's pregnant before everyone else. It's harder than I thought to keep a secret from family, especially one as big as the Laurel Springs Emergency Response Team. I never actually realized how up in each other's business we all are.

"Shit." She sits up from where she's lounging. "What am I gonna do if somebody hands me a glass of champagne. People know I drink. They'll never believe I'm not doing it just because I want to be sober for my wedding night. People know

Ransom and I, they know we get freaky once we've had a few drinks. How are we going to pull this off, Kels? Am I crazy for even trying?"

There's only one thing for me to do. This is my best friend in the entire world, she's listened to every doubt I've ever had, she's cheered with each moment I hit a goal, and right now she needs me. In the grand scheme of things, what I'm offering isn't huge, but it's something I can do for her. "Hand it to me, I'll take care of it for you, and make sure you have sparkling cider all night. We've got this. Your wedding and reception are going to go off without a hitch Stella, I swear."

"Are you sure?" she asks. "You drink, but not as much as me."

"I can handle this, Stelle, I promise. I've got this."

Fucking famous last words.

TWO

Nick

Love is a promise delivered, already broken. That's what I learned from the first half of my life. Love hurts, it breaks up families, it brings unhappiness and pain, disappointment and sorrow. Love doesn't save, it steals. Anything and everything worth having.

But watching Ransom and Stella as they dance around their reception, seeing how happy they are. Watching the smile covering both of their faces, the way my best friend holds my sister in his arms? It makes me wonder if I'm the broken one, and everyone else knows the answer to the secret. There's a part of me that thinks I'm wrong, because I see successful couples all around me. The difference in those couples and what I've been a part of? Me. I'm always the common denominator, and after a while – you come to realize how bad you are loving anyone else, including yourself.

Sighing, I bring my bottle of beer up to my lips, taking a drink. It's nasty, because I've been nursing the same one all night. I'm not much of a drinker, given the way I grew up. Loud words and hard fists were the only things that came from drinking. But those thoughts have no business being in such a happy place tonight.

"Nick." I hear a giggle. "Niiiiccckkk."

A slight smile spreads across my face as I look to my left. I'd know that voice anywhere, and honestly nine times out of ten, no matter what she says, she makes me smile. "What's up, Kels?"

She leans back against the wall next to me. "I'm so drunk," she laughs. "I've been drinking all of Stella's alcohol so no one knows she's pregnant," she sighs, tilting her head back, closing her eyes. "Damn I'm dizzy."

I watch her sway, even though the wall does its best to hold her up. Turning to face her, I set my drink on a nearby table and proceed to block her in. One hand at the wall above her head, another near her waist. Locking her gaze with mine, I ask a very important question. "Who's driving you home?"

"You?" She gives me a silly grin, before her tongue sneaks out, wiping at her lip. Fuck if I don't feel things I shouldn't right now. "Or Tucker." She points to the K-9 trainer for the Laurel Springs Police Department. "He's been talking to me all night. He's super nice." She wrinkles her nose.

My stomach cramps as I think of her going home with someone who isn't me tonight. Even though I know Tucker and Karsyn are in some kind of friends with benefits thing, it still leaves a bad taste in my mouth. There's no way I want to look closer into that thought and figure out why, and before I know it, I'm offering. "I'll take you home," I assure her.

"Do you care if we go now?" She tilts her head to the side before bringing them back to mine. Her dark eyes shine brightly with the effects of the alcohol she's had tonight, her cheeks are a bright pink.

"You don't want to stay to see them off?" It kind of catches me off-guard, especially when a sadness washes across her face. I figured she'd be here until the very end.

"Nope." She holds up the bouquet she caught earlier. It's beautiful, handmade by one of my mom's best friends. It looks almost as beautiful as her in this muted light. "Already got what I came for. A tradition that'll stop with me."

I should stop myself, but I'm a glutton for punishment. "Why do you think the tradition will stop with you?"

Those bleary eyes look up at me, the side of her mouth tilting up in a sad smile. "Because I know you, and you're never gonna wanna get married. Especially to someone like me."

Love. It breaks your heart, right? Every fucking time. The worst part? I can't even deny it, can't even give her just a little bit of damn hope, because I know myself. All I'll do is disappoint her and push her away until she wants absolutely nothing to do with me.

"C'mon Kels, let's get out of here."

Grabbing her hand in mine, I help her walk out, focusing on making sure she doesn't fall in the high heels she's wearing. I wave at a couple of people we know and signal to Caleb I'm making sure his sister gets home okay, but I feel like a bastard right now.

What she said was true, and even though I'd give anything to change it, I know I can't.

Kelsea

Didn't even respond when I made the comment about how he wouldn't wanna get married to anyone, including me. I may be drunk, but I'm not stupid. Those words were said to gauge the reaction in Nick. Sadly, there wasn't a reaction. At least not an outwardly one. I have this feeling Nick keeps everything he feels inside. If people don't know what he cares about, they can't hurt him. I've known him for years, have watched as he's tried to keep things from me, women, bad habits, details from his past, but nothing has ever driven me away. Whether Nick knows it or not, he needs me, we need each other.

I'm quiet as he drives to my apartment. The early March weather is cooler than normal, a slight drizzle falls, kissing the windshield. It's just enough so that the lights of other cars look like a kaleidoscope in the darkness. It makes me dizzy again, so I lean my head against the cool passenger window and close my eyes, sighing as I snuggle down in his leather seats, thankful for the relief.

"Are you okay, Kels?"

He actually sounds like he cares, actually sounds as if he's worried about me. I take that tone and wrap it around my body like a blanket. It's not very often he lets his guard down enough to even give me this much. One of the perks of loving a man who doesn't believe in it.

"I'm tired, Nick. It's been a long day."

And now I'm lying. The day has been long, but I'm also tired of being no one to him. Of being the person he contacts when he's lonely and doesn't want to be by himself, but then him not responding when I tell him my feelings. I'm so tired of it all. I just want one night, with his arms around me. To know what it feels like for him to lose control with me. God, I want it so bad I can taste it. The worst part about it is, I feel like I deserve it. I've seen him at his worst, why can't I get him at his best, too?

"It has been a long day." He reaches over, squeezing my thigh with his hand. Slightly, I part my knees, hoping he gets the idea of where I want his hand to go. "Who knew we'd have so much to do, and we're not even the ones who got married."

"Yeah." I smile, thinking back to how happy my friends

were. "But it was totally worth it because it was so beautiful. They're going to have an amazing life together."

"Yeah," he answers as he pulls into the parking lot of my complex. "They will." He puts his car in park. We're both silent. I wish I knew what he was thinking, wish I could tell him exactly what I'm thinking. But this is us, this is our relationship, and it's how it's always been. "Let me walk you up, make sure everything's okay."

This is the part that bothers me. When he acts like I matter. I know better than to argue with him, so I wait for him to come around to my side of the car, opening my door for me. He helps me out, and as he walks me up the steps to where my apartment is, his hand is on the small of my back. There's a heat that I always feel when he touches me, but tonight, it feels hotter. It's a brand on my skin.

"Give me your keys, Kels."

Fumbling in my bag, I do my best to locate them, but I can't see inside. Even if I could, I have a feeling everything would be blurry. I really drank more than I meant to. "I'm looking for them."

Carefully he takes my bag out of my hand, fishing the keys out. He's quick and efficient as he unlocks the door, slightly pushing me inside.

"You should leave a light on," he says quietly as he goes over to where my lamp is, turning it on.

"I forgot with all the running around today. Taking care of me was the last thing on my mind."

We're quiet again, staring at one another. His dark eyes smolder as he looks at me, an intensity I'm not prepared for, but one I would take as long as it's pointed toward me.

"You want me to stay while you change and stuff? You've had a lot to drink tonight."

Truth is I don't want him to leave. I never want him to leave. "If you don't mind."

"Whatever you need."

He's as comfortable here as he is in his own apartment. When Stella lived here, he was here all the time, and he's here at least a few times a week with me. It's almost as if he can't stand to be with me, but he can't stand to not be with me either. Which confuses the hell out of me all the time. A thought crosses my mind, one that wouldn't normally cross it, but tonight I'm tired.

Tired of being the person who doesn't get what she wants. Instead I want to be the person who takes what she needs. Turning so that my back is presented to him, I move my curls out of the way. "Do you mind unzipping me? It's going to be a pain in the ass for me to do it on my own, and I don't want to rip the dress. I'd like to return it and get my deposit back."

I can hear his intake of breath. "How did you get it on?"

"Stella helped me." I look over my shoulder, back at him, lowering my eyes in what I hope is a flirtatious stare. When I can hear him inhale a deep breath, I think maybe I succeeded.

He stands, towering over me now that I've kicked off my high heels. His hands are warm as he situates me so he can find the zipper. It feels like this moment takes forever, the only sound in the room is the tines of the zipper releasing as he pulls it downward. The coolness of the air in the apartment tells me exactly how much of my bare back he's exposed, and slight bumps dot my skin.

I shiver when his hands push my dress apart, can hear his groan when my bare back is exposed to him. "Son of a bitch, Kels. You've gone through this whole day with no bra on?"

"The dress is tight, so the adhesive one worked just fine." My voice is soft, afraid I'm going to break whatever spell this is. He's never talked to me with this roughness around the edges of his tone, never sounded like he was in pain from not touching me.

"Adhesive?" he questions.

Gathering all my courage, I reach up, pull the dress down in front of me, and then turn around to face him. His gaze is locked to the nude colored adhesive cups that hold my skin from his gaze. Reaching forward I grab his hand, bringing it to the edge of the material.

"All you have to do is pull it off, Nick. It's completely up to you."

As I watch him, his face giving away nothing, I pray that this won't be another embarrassment I'll have to endure. I hope with everything I have, I finally get to taste the forbidden fruit of the man standing in front of me.

THREE

Nick

The devil on my right shoulder is completely at odds with the angel on the left. He's telling me to take what I want, she's telling me to do what I know is right. Me? I'm at odds. For once to not be the guy who doesn't think he deserves shit. I've been denying myself for so long, but at the same time, I've also been denying Kelsea what she wants and what she deserves.

"Take it, Nick," she whispers, holding her palm against mine. Her eyes are closed as she continues whispering the words almost like a prayer. "Please, just take it."

In the end, it's not because of my needs and wants, it's the desperation in her voice, the way it catches on the last word that rocks me out of my stupor. It's the fact she still wants me, no matter how many times I've hurt her, no matter how much I've pushed her away. It's the fact she's never given up on me. Even when I've given up on myself.

A groan is ripped from the back of my throat, coming out on just this side of a growl as my fingers curl against the material at her breast. Her hand drops, letting me pull what looks to be a big sticker off. And when I do, I can't stand not seeing the other one bared to my gaze, too. Reaching over, I dispose of it, leaving her naked for my eyes only from the waist up. My hand shakes as I use my thumb and index finger to cup the underside, plumping it up so that her nipple stands out in relief from the rest of her body. I can't help it, I lick my lips like I'm about to have my favorite ice cream on a mother fuckin' hot day. Her hooded eyes watch me behind black as night, fuck-me-until-I-can't-scream-anymore lashes. She must have done something for the wedding because I've never seen them so alluring, never seen her green eyes pop so beautifully against the backdrop of her face.

"I can stop." My promise is a broken whisper, leaning forward so that my lips are a breath away. "Any time, I can stop. Just say the word."

She grabs hold of my hair, threading her fingers through it, tugging me to her puckered skin. I fight against her hold slightly, blowing a breath through my lips, enjoying the tightening of her flesh in response. Risking one more glance up at her, I capture her nub in between my lips, using my tongue to apply pressure as I lick against the hardness. Swirling, coaxing, daring to unleash the vixen hiding behind the Kelsea she's supposed to be for everyone else. Bastard I may be, but I want something for myself. These moments between us? They don't belong to anyone else.

"Nick," she gasps, her knees going weak as she pulls my hair tighter. Her nails scrape across my scalp, the slight pain making my cock jump in reaction. "Oh my mmmm, shit..." She thrusts herself at me, feeding me those magnificent tits I've always admired but never dreamed would be mine, but she's falling and I'm having a hard time keeping up.

Bending at the waist, I push my hands down her sides, slide

along her hips, and grip her ass tightly. I grunt as I lift her, pushing her thighs around my waist. I have a one-track mind as I walk us into her bedroom, tossing her on the cover. Abandoning her chest, I realize if this may be the only time I get her, I'm going to take everything I want.

Hitting my knees on the carpet, I grasp her lace panties in my fingers, yanking, feeling satisfaction when I hear the material give. Throwing them behind me, I grab hold of her hips, hauling her down to me, bringing my face in between her thighs.

"Nick, nobody," she stops, as I glance up, our eyes meeting.

"Are you a virgin?" I croak, my throat dry as I think about being her initiation, but truth is, if I am, I am. As much as it scares me, it would be my honor.

"No." She reaches up, twisting her nipple in between her forefinger and thumb. Tilting her head back as she enjoys the passion for a moment, before looking back down at me. "I've only been with two other guys, but no one..." She gets shy, trying to close her thighs to my gaze.

"Never went downtown, huh?" I can't help but feel my chest puff out. I'm great at this, and I know I am. In high school, it was how I got so many girls to give me a shot. Of course I'm not going to tell her that.

"No." She shakes her head, looking embarrassed. "Never."

"Relax, Kels," I put my hand on her hipbone, holding her down. "I got this."

Kelsea

Nick wasn't lying. As I lay ten minutes later panting against my bed, aftershocks of the best orgasm I've ever had rocking my body. I don't even know what to say as I watch him stand up, wipe his mouth off with the back of his hand, and untuck the button-down he's wearing. His movements are agitated and jerky. When he turns to the side, and I see what he's rocking in his dress pants, I know exactly why he's agitated.

We watch each other, neither of us saying anything, but I'm still breathing hard as I take in the way he undresses himself. It's like a strip show, only for me. His hands go to his waistband, yanking his leather belt apart, pulling it from his belt loops. His fingers are impossibly long and shaking as he fights with the button and zipper, pushing them down with an impatience I'm feeling too.

"Are you sure?" he asks, his voice hoarse, his eyes impossibly dark as he stares at me in the dimness of the nightlight in the room. His big body is on alert as he stares down at me, his forearms tense and relax as he waits for me to give him the affirmative.

"Yeah." I open my arms to him, licking my suddenly dry lips. "I want you, Nick."

He lets out a slow breath, pushing his hand down his flat stomach, before he reaches into the waistband of his boxer briefs. Given the motion, I can tell he's giving himself a few strokes. His head falls backward, and I'm greeted with the sight of his strong neck, prominent Adam's apple as he gives himself a few moments of pleasure. When he speaks, his voice is all gravel and deep tones. "Are you on birth control, Kels?"

"No." I shake my head. "No reason to be."

His head gives a terse nod as he bends, fishing his wallet out of his pants pocket. I watch as he finally pushes the boxer briefs down, grips his cock with a strong hand, and then opens the condom with his teeth. I almost come again as I watch him spread the latex down his length. The way it jumps at his touch, the way his forearm tightens, his abs tighten as he stops for a minute, closing his eyes and moaning. He's a man who enjoys physical pleasure, and for me there's nothing sexier. "It's been a while, Kels, but I'll make it good for you."

The fact it's been a while for him makes me crazily happy. In my mind I think about him waiting for me. Maybe he was celibate because he was waiting on the moment he and I could be together. Even though I know it isn't true, I cling to the thought with both hands, hoping it doesn't disappear.

He crawls onto the bed, over my body, licking my stomach, paying attention to the nipples he abandoned earlier, nipping at my neck and jawline until he's even with my lips.

"Wanna kiss you, more than I've ever wanted anything."

It sounds like those words are ripped from his throat, and maybe they are, because they show emotion and anyone who knows him knows emotion isn't his strong suit. We stare at one another for long minutes. I can see something there, a glimmer of hope, of what could be if he'd just let himself feel. If he'd let me in. It's too much, I'm feeling way too much right now.

"Kiss me." I wrap my arms around his neck, bringing my mouth up to his. When he opens, his tongue tangling with mine, and I taste myself there. It's not as unpleasant as I always thought it would be. I dig my fingers into his back, wanting to be closer to him, wanting him to own me.

His hands grip the covers beside my head as he grinds into me. "Wanna fuck you, baby."

Baby. He called me baby. He's never called me baby. I hold the endearment in my pocket, tucking it away for a cold day. Going from someone who never thought they'd have any piece of Nick Kepler, to what's going on right now? I kinda want to pinch myself and pray I won't wake up.

"Please," I beg, thrusting against him.

He lets go of the cover with his left hand, holding himself up with the right. Stronger than I ever imagined he was, he brings the left hand down between my legs, testing my core against the invasion of his fingers. I moan as he curls his index finger inside me, touching a hot spot, one that makes me thrust harder against him.

"So wet, so hot, so fucking tight." He drops his head into my neck, mouthing at my skin as he pulls his fingers from their haven.

That's when he thrusts home, and I have a feeling of belonging like I've never had before. I hold on tightly to him as he swings his hips in and out, back and forth, bumping, grinding against me. He holds on tightlyto the covers as he uses the fabric to help him set his pace. There aren't any words between us, only the sounds of two people going after their physical release. I'm moaning each time he pushes and pulls, he's grunting with each thrust. Sweat drips down my face, it covers his chest and back, making it hard for me to grip his muscles. My legs are tight around his waist, digging my heels into his back as I feel myself start to build again.

"Ahhh." His mouth is right next to my ear, his teeth nipping, his tongue soothing. I close my eyes tightly, imagining what he looks like, letting him sweep me away with the feelings of him deep inside me. I'm drunk on lust, drowsy on passion, and one hundred percent here for whatever this man wants to do to me. "Never felt this goddamn good before, baby."

I can't even answer him as I feel his arms wrap completely around my body, hugging me close. My thighs widen as much as they can, I cross my ankles at the small of his back, hold tightly to his neck as he thrusts with abandon into me. Our bodies slap against one another, a vulgar sound in the otherwise quiet room, and God help me, but it turns me on.

"Come for me, Nick," I whisper in his ear, giving him a little nip of my own. Plastering myself against his body, wanting to feel every little nuance he has. Who knows if I'll ever get this chance again.

It's a guttural yell as he plunges deep, letting go, yelling, cursing through it as he empties into me. When he lays his mouth against my neck, sucking harshly, I'm surprised by another fall into pleasure.

As the two of us pant, arms wrapped tightly around each other, I think to myself nothing will ever be more perfect in my life again.

FOUR

Kelsea

I'm fighting to open my eyes as I hear rustling the next morning. To be honest, I'm surprised he's still here. Given what I know about him, I figured he'd take the chance to slip away in the dead of the night. Tiredness washes over my body, along with a relaxation I haven't felt in months. There's even a soreness, courtesy of what I spent the night doing. The stress of helping Stella get married and my worry over Nick has finally caught up with me as I sink further against my mattress.

"Kels." I hear a deep voice whispering in my ear. I feel the scratch of a beard on my shoulder.

"Hmmm?" I stretch, before burrowing deeply into the arms wrapped around me.

Moist lips land on my bare shoulder before the heat of his breath pulses against me. "I have to be at work in an hour, but I don't want to go."

"I don't want you to go either," I whisper as he tightens his arms around me. Pressing myself against him, I feel his hard length at my back.

"So that's how it's going to be? You're going to make it hard for me to leave?" The words are gruff as he kisses my neck.

Feeling a little ornery, I tilt my head to the side, giving him free access to the flesh he's mouthing. "That's not the only thing hard."

He chuckles loud enough that I can feel the rumble against my back. "Damn right about that."

His hands cup my breasts from behind, his fingers plucking at my nipples, while I arch back against him. "Nick." I let it out on a sigh.

His voice is deep as he commands. "Roll over." His hands move down my stomach, latching onto my hips, pushing me over onto my front.

Reaching up with my hands, I grab hold of the top of the mattress as his hand moves down my back. A sensual stroke from my neck, to the dip in my waist, making me shiver, making my core clench. Cupping his hands over my hip bones, he jerks slightly. "Face down, ass up, Kels."

My eyes close as I hear the aroused tone of his voice. This is another one of those things I haven't done much, and I love the way his body dwarfs mine, that I feel so small underneath him. Lifting my hips off the mattress, I grip the edge as I wait to see what he's going to do. He moans deep in his throat as I feel his big palm slap against my ass, the bite of his fingers in the flesh as he takes a handful. My eyes roll back in my head as his fingertips move down, pushing into my wet heat.

He presses two fingers in between my thighs, opening and stretching, rubbing as I feel my body responding to his. Moaning, I bury my head in my pillow.

"You can be loud, baby, nobody gonna hear you but me."

He leans forward so that I can feel the heat of his body, the rasp of that stubble against my skin. With more strength than I realize he has, he situates me, rubbing his cock against my wet heat. Nick pushes inside of me as I gasp loudly. "Oh my God, you feel so big this way."

"It's because I am." His words are a grunt as I feel him push in and pull out.

Already the two of us are sweating, his stomach sliding against my back. "Don't stop," I beg.

He breathes heavily when his forehead drops to my back, and his hips stop their movement. "Fuck, you feel good."

"So do you." I press back against him. Turning so that I can see him over my shoulder. "Please don't stop."

"Can't stop," he gasps. "Won't stop," he pants. "Woke up with morning wood, you against me, and I knew I wouldn't be able to leave here without a final taste of you."

"You never have to leave without a taste of me," I tell him, hoping he hears what I'm trying to tell him. There's no reason he has to think this is the end.

"Fuck, I can't get deep enough." He reaches up, grasping my hair in his hand, yanking roughly.

No one has ever done this before, and an excited scream leaves my mouth. "Holy shit, Nick," I moan, feeling my nipples peak harder, tighter, my heartbeat kicks up faster. "Harder!"

"Kelsea, son of a bitch, the condom broke," he grunts.

"Don't care, keep going," I push back against him, gasping. "Please, keep going."

Wrapping my hair around his fist, he does as I ask, using my hair to help him plunge in and pull out, making my knees widen against the sheet. I'm slipping, slipping, until his knees hook inside mine, pushing them as wide as they can go. I'm almost lying flat against the mattress as he covers me, fucking me, rutting at me like I'd imagine animals going at each other.

"Feels so goddamn good," he grunts into my ear as he

thrusts, making noise each time he bottoms out. "You feel better than anyone else ever has."

There's a pride I feel in what he's said, and I let myself bask in it for a moment. But then he's riding me hard, pressing my clit against the sheet. Before I realize what's happening, I feel my body tighten, and I scream out my orgasm as I feel the heat of his release emptying inside me. The two of us are panting, writhing against each other, and as I'm pressed fully into the mattress, his heart thudding against mine, I hear him sigh.

"What do we need to do? Is this a time you could be pregnant?" He questions.

When that sentence doesn't scare the hell out of me, I know for sure I am completely and totally in love with this man. But I'm also aware that there was fear in his voice.

"It's okay, I can get Plan B at work," I intentionally soothe the fear I heard.

"Are you sure?"

"Positive, I don't think either of us are ready for a baby right now," even though I would figure it out with him.

"Sounds good," he kisses my shoulder softly.

"Yeah," I trail off. "Sounds good..."

FIVE

Nick

"Running late today?"

Immediately I'm on the defensive as I hear Kelsea's dad, and my boss, Menace speak to me, even though I can hear the teasing lilt in his voice. I'm almost an hour late, I haven't showered since the wedding, and I have a three-day-old beard which isn't like me at all. But I can't tell him where I've been, what I've been doing. The only person I respect more than him is my dad, so I attempt to take his teasing in stride.

"Just a little." I hurry to see if there's any info in my mailbox, doing my best to not meet his eyes.

"I think we're all a little slower than normal after the wedding last night. Did you get Kels home alright? Caleb said you were taking her when I asked."

It's an innocent question. Something any dad would ask about his daughter, but I immediately feel guilty. He's my superior who's always treated me with respect and supported anything I've set out to do in my job. But I'm also not prepared to tell him how I spent last night and this morning. "Yeah, I got her home, made sure she had what she needed, and then left."

"Thanks for doing that. Rina and I were having a good time."

I can tell by the way he smirks they had more than a good time. He and Kari have the kind of marriage my mom and dad do. If I was to ever get married, theirs is the kind of marriage I want. Them, coupled with Ransom and Stella, they do give me hope one day I can be normal.

"All of us were, it was a great wedding."

It's surprising saying those words doesn't feel wrong. Ransom and Stella are meant to be, and they're going to live an amazing life together. I don't know what else to say, so I opt to make a quick getaway. "Gotta get going." I hook my thumb out to where our patrol cars are parked.

"Be safe out there, Nick."

Nodding, I give him a wave. "Always am."

When I get into my patrol car, what I like to call my office, I finally feel right. I'm not nervous, not doubting who I am as a person. This right here is where I feel good about myself. As I get checked in, listening to what's coming over the radio, my phone makes the sound of a notification.

K: I had a great time with you. Maybe we can do it again?

My hands literally shake as I hold the phone. After the way we heated up the sheets together, I know we mesh well. The question is am I willing to give us a shot? Thinking back to how Ransom looked at Stella last night, I think maybe I am.

N: Maybe we can. Let me text you when I get off-shift.

K: Be safe out there!

The smile that spreads across my face is one I'm not accustomed to. It's been a long time since I've felt happiness like this. A really fucking long time. If I'm not mistaken it's almost a giddiness – and that is shit I've never felt. Starting my car, I begin my route through Laurel Springs. The first few hours pass by uneventful; I pull over a few people for going too fast, but then a call comes over the radio. It's one I hear, but don't really hear. I need it repeated, to make sure I heard correctly.

"Dispatch, come again?"

"We have a welfare check requested on a child, called in by Laurel Springs Elementary this afternoon."

Immediately my stomach clenches; it feels like I've just gone over the drop off while riding a roller coaster. My pulse pounds, picking up speed just like that roller coaster. "Did they let the child go home?"

"Yes, there was some confusion about the course of action that needed to be taken, and in that confusion he was let on the bus and sent home. Which is why they're requesting a home visit, rather than going to the school."

I make sure my finger is off the radio. "Son of a bitch, what the fuck with these people?" Unfortunately I know from experience how most well-meaning people are. They're well-meaning until it's time to take action. The only people who ever followed through for me were the Keplers and that's one hundred percent the reason I call them Mom and Dad now. Keying the radio, I answer. "Give me the address and show me responding."

The address comes through on the laptop sitting to my side. That roller coaster ride in my stomach comes to a complete stop. Saliva pools against my tongue and I fight against my gag reflex. Fuck me. That's the same neighborhood I lived in when I was a kid. It's actually three houses down from the one I grew up in. There are good people in the neighborhood, but they are few and far between. Most are drug addicts, alcoholics, and people who seem to think life owes them something they haven't yet been given. They don't believe in trying to do better for themselves. They believe in waiting for someone to hand them the proverbial dream, instead of working for it. This is the place were complacency rules and dreams come to die. Women who think they'll be with baby daddy forever, and two months later they're single, trying to figure out how to make ends meet.

As I park, I advise dispatch I've arrived at the residence, preparing myself for what's about to take place. "Can you get me another unit headed this way? I have a feeling I'm gonna need it."

"10-4." I hear the voice of Kelsea's brother. "I'm about five minutes away. I'll be there."

Shit. Getting out, I casually rest my hand on the butt of my gun. Glancing around, I feel the melancholy of this place, it's beating down on me like rain in a summer thunderstorm. This home is unhappy, and it doesn't take a psychic to see it. It's in disrepair; the brick is faded, the walk leading up to the house looks like it once was concrete, but now it's just a worn patch of grass. When I get to the entrance, I notice the storm door is hanging off the hinges. Carefully opening it, I knock on the wooden one. This is one of the most nerve-wracking parts of my job, not knowing what's about to happen. This situation could be numerous ways, and I understand that.

"Laurel Springs Police, open up!" I try again when no one answers my first attempt to make contact.

I'm shifting my feet, getting irritated as I wait when the door opens. The man standing there looks so much like the man I left at fifteen, I have to do a double-take and remind myself this isn't the man my mom was with back then. All assholes tend to look the same.

"Can I help you?" he snarls.

Dude's body language is throwing off a ton of signals to me.

His eyes are squinted, face flushed, and when I glance down at his hands, noticing they're clenched into fists. Dip rests between his lip and teeth, and I just know this fucker is going to spit on my shoes.

"Are you the father of Darren Metcalfe?" I check the name I wrote down in my notebook before I got out of my cruiser.

"Yeah, what's he done now?"

Exactly what I expected. "He's not done anything, but I would like to see him if that's alright with you."

He looks like he wants to say no, and I wonder if he's going to lie to me, but right when I'm about to give up, he turns around, bellowing the boy's name. The two of us wait, both staring down one another. When the boy comes to where we stand, he looks up at me, I look down at him, and I see myself. I see everything about the kid I was in the eyes of this child. Caleb arrives, coming to stand beside me, allowing me to take the child off to the side, while he talks to the father.

"I'm Officer Nick Kepler with the Laurel Springs Police Department," I tell him as he looks up at me with big eyes. "I grew up right over there." I point to the house that had been my hell as a child.

Me admitting that is a game changer, and I can tell. He relaxes, his posture stoops, and his eyes lose much of the deer-in-the-headlights look. "And you're a cop now?"

"I'm a cop now." I nod, giving him a small smile. "And because I'm a cop, I'm here to protect you when things get rough." I raise my eyebrow. "Are things rough around here?"

He looks down, kicking at the broken concrete of the driveway. "Yeah." I strain to hear his small voice.

"Things were rough for me too, when I lived over there. Never had the cool clothes that all my friends had, never had enough food to feel full, never enough money to go on field trips with my friends."

His gaze meets mine, understanding shining brightly. This child gets where I'm coming from, because he's living the life I did. I purposely don't mention the abuse. I need him to come around and tell me that himself.

"How are things rough?" It's important that I don't coach him, that he tells me on his own. "Has someone hurt you?"

Tears pool in his brown eyes, his bottom lip fucking trembling, breaking my goddamn heart. When he nods, I want to beat the fucker in the doorway. "Can you show me?"

Slowly he lifts up the sleeve of his shirt, showing blue and black bruises in the shape of fingerprints.

"Is that it?" I do my best to keep my anger out of my voice, because I don't want to scare this kid. He's had enough fear in his life.

He shakes his head, pulling up the hem of his t-shirt, various bruises in stages of healing can be seen.

"Who did this to you?"

Tears stream down his face. I can't help it, I reach down, brushing them away. "It's okay to cry." I reach into my car, getting a tissue, before handing it to him. "It doesn't make you weak to cry."

"My dad," he sobs. "My dad hurt me."

He throws himself at me, his little arms tight around my waist. I don't know how old this kid is, but he's definitely on the small side. Putting my hands on his back, I look up, making eye contact with Caleb. Nodding, I give him the go-ahead to put the dad in cuffs. After getting Darren situated in the front of my patrol car with a stuffed animal that I keep in the trunk of my car for these situations, I place a call to child services and then walk down to where Caleb has his dad cuffed.

"Why'd you do it?" I question.

"You're Nick Cooper." Recognition shows across his face.

I haven't been called that in a long time, and I honestly don't know how to react, except to say, "No. I'm Nick Kepler."

"No, you're Nick Cooper, you grew up over there." He tilts his head to the house I've been running from for over half my life.

"I'm Officer Nickolas Kepler," I repeat.

He continues. "If anyone should understand what's going on here, it's you. We all repeat the sins of the father, don't we?"

Meaning his dad beat the shit out of him and now he's doing it to his own kid.

"Put him in the car," I tell Caleb, barely keeping the disgust out of my tone.

And all those good feelings I had earlier, about maybe where I could go with Kels? They're gone, because now I see that no matter how hard we try, we just can't outrun our past.

SIX

Kelsea

"Hey!" I wave to Ruby as I throw my purse down on her couch. "Where are the kids?"

"Kari took them to karate." She grins. "So that means we get to have adult food and adult conversation tonight. I have that wine you and Stella introduced me to. Want a glass?"

"Don't mind if I do. It's been a long day, even if I didn't have to work." I grin back at her. I love my niece and nephew, but sometimes they completely overtake every situation they're in. Tonight I'm just wanting to have a relaxing time. Before I can say anything, Caleb comes through the door.

"Ladies," he greets us both.

I'm almost jealous when he snakes his arms around her waist, kissing at her neck, grabbing her ear between his teeth. The two of them have such an intoxicating passion and such an all-encompassing chemistry, it forces those around them to pay attention. Deep in my gut I know the way they look at each other is what I want, what I deserve. Right next to the feeling is the fear I may never get to experience it.

She spins in his arms. "How was your day?" Ruby asks him as she stands on her tiptoes, leaning in for a kiss.

His arms tighten around her. "Fuckin' brutal. Nick and I had to do a welfare check on a kid, and CPS got called."

Immediately I'm all ears. Hearing his name, along with the fact CPS was involved, makes me worry. "Are you okay?" I ask my brother, hoping he realizes I'm asking for Nick too.

The way he looks at me – suspicious with a bit of compassion – tells me he knows exactly why I'm asking.

"I'm good. Pissed at the situation, but Nick was real quiet after it happened. Have to think it reminded him of his situation."

"At least the kid had someone there who could relate." Ruby rubs his shoulders, grabbing his hand before she kisses his bicep.

The way she tucks herself in beside him almost makes me want to cry. When Caleb comes home after a rough night, she's there to help him forget, to make him feel better. Whose there for Nick?

Nobody, because he tends to be a loaner. While I know that's on him, it still makes me sad. Instead of forgetting his past, he's forced to face it head on.

"Yeah, anyway I'm gonna go get changed."

Clearing the emotion out of my throat, I'm overly happy as I hope to hide how upset I am. "I'll set the table."

More than anything, I need to keep myself busy. If I don't, I'll make a fool out of myself and this thing with Nick is way too new for me to fuck it up before it even begins.

AS I WATCH THE CLOCK, I become more and more disappointed. I know for a fact Nick got off-shift a few hours ago. We've had dinner already and I know he's avoiding me. The old Kelsea would have left him to his own devices, not wanting to rock the boat. This Kelsea, she's going to take a chance and go for what she wants. Tired of waiting, I send a text.

K: Hey, I'm at Caleb's, heard you had a hard day today. Are you off yet?

"You okay today?" Ruby asks as I help her do the dishes since she cooked for us. "You seem a little sad."

Sighing, I think about telling her everything, but I honestly don't want the sympathy I know I'll see in her eyes. I've seen it too many times from Stella, and I can't see it from my sister-in-law. "Just tired." I make light of it. "Last night was a long night, couple with a long day and the months leading up to the wedding. Just catching up with me."

"But it was fun." She grins as she bumps me with her hip. "Caleb and I got a little drunk. We actually called an Uber to bring us home." Her cheeks are a slight pink as she lowers her voice, giggling before she speaks. "Then we fucked in the living room since the kids were at my parents' house. Do you know how long it's been since we've been able to do something like that?"

"Oh my God, Ruby," I gasp with shock, even though I finish with a laugh. "I hate hearing that about my brother, but I'm so glad you had a good time." I dry the dish she hands to me.

"It was super nice." She closes her eyes, biting her lip. She shivers slightly before she gives me another dish. "Didn't I see you leave with Nick?"

Shit. I can't give nonverbal clues like she just did. They would totally give me away, and I'm not prepared for my brother and dad to know what happened after we left. "Yeah, he took me home."

"Anything happen with him?" She raises an eyebrow. Usually she can read me like a book, but I have to keep this locked down. She'll have questions that I won't have answers for. "Hmmm?"

Again I think about telling her everything, but how can I tell her something when I don't even know what's going on. "Nope, he was a perfect gentleman.

A frown mars her pretty face, along with a look of compassion. She's feeling sorry for me as I hear the words coming out of her mouth. "Aww, Kels."

"No, I'm fine." I stop her from giving me a pacifying answer. "Really, I'm fine."

Drying my hands off, I grab my cell. Still no message from Nick. My fingers shake as I send him another text. I'm irritated at the both of us. Him because he won't answer, and me because I care so much.

K: I'm just worried about you. Are you okay?

Thirty minutes later, as I'm leaving Caleb's I still don't have an answer.

K: No matter what you're going through, Nick, I can help you, but only if you let me.

Nick

I should answer the messages Kelsea is sending me, I know I should. If I'm being honest, I want to, but at the same time I want to protect her. From myself.

I don't know how I tricked the Keplers into adopting me. I'll never know how I won that lottery. It feels like I used up all my good juju with them. Nothing else in my life has ever gone so right.

My friendship with Ransom notwithstanding, I somehow always manage to push people away. And in always doing that, I did what I didn't want to do with Kels. The one thing I've never wanted to do to her is be a dick, but I can't seem to make myself be the guy I know I can be. Every time I pick up my phone to answer her, I just don't fucking know what to say. No, that's a lie. I want to say too much, and I'm not ready to do that yet. Maybe she's also not ready to hear it either.

It's nights like this I hate living alone, but at the same time I hate being around other people. The only thing saving me is routine. I can do it with muscle memory. I don't have to think. I'm not required to be responsible, all I have to do is what I know I'm supposed to.

First thing: take off my gear, store my gun.

Second thing: take a shower.

Third thing: eat something I've meal prepped earlier in the week, for nights like this when I can't get out of my own head.

The routine is over now, and I have nothing but the thoughts in my head. If Ransom were in town, I'd head over to his and Stella's house, play with Rambo, but they aren't. Rambo is at my parent's house, and if I go there, I'll have to tell them what's going on inside my head. That's not my idea of a good time right now. No matter how close I am to them, I've never let them be privy to the voices swirling when I don't have anything to keep my mind busy.

Blowing out an agitated breath, I sit on my couch, turning the television on, mindlessly searching for something to watch, but the memories won't stop. They're loud, louder than they've been in a long time. Compliments of my last call of the night.

"What happened to it, Nick?" His voice is harsh, eyes dark as night, hulking over me, knowing he's bigger, knowing he's intimidating.

The man in front of me is a living monster. When I get old enough and big enough, I'm going to hurt him like he's hurt me. Make him cry like he's made me. He's not my real dad, he tells me that often. My real dad passed away, and according to anyone who talks about my mom, she's had a wheel of men rolling in and out of her life since. Every single night I wonder how my life would be different if my dad were still alive.

"I...I..I don't know." I fumble with my words. The fucking stutter that shows up when he questions me, the thing that makes him angry.

"What do you mean you don't know? You were the last person to use it." He holds up the power screwdriver in front of my face.

"N...N...No, I wasn't." I shake my head. "Jase was the last person to use it," I mention his son. "He u...us...us...used it last night."

"Well guess what? I asked him, and he told me you did this. You know what that means, it's time for your punishment."

Sweat breaks out across my forehead, my hands begin to shake, and I fight against my gag reflex as my stomach churns. I'm fourteen, and I'm tall, but I'm small for my age, because I haven't had proper nutrition my whole life. As I watch him take off his belt, jerking it from each loop and holding it in his hand, I feel anger. Anger at him, at my mom, at my situation, and I hate it. I hate it all.

More than once I've wondered what would happen if I hurt myself. Would the world be better if I weren't here? I've researched it. It wouldn't be hard. A few too many of the pills mom likes to keep in her bedroom, maybe the gun this fucker keeps under his pillow, or throwing myself in front of traffic. I've thought of all the ways I can make myself disappear, but every time I try, I cry. I cry because I feel like there's something else out there for me. What? I don't know, but I have to believe I wasn't born for this.

As he brings his arm down, the belt in his hand, I reach out, wrapping the leather around my forearm, yanking roughly. I yank so hard, he falls down, flat on his face. When he looks up at me, hate and anger glittering in his eyes. I know I won't be going to school until the bruises heal.

"Fuck," I growl in disgust as I turn the TV off, throwing the remote on the couch. "When does this shit just go away?" I question, putting my hands on my head.

Here, inside this apartment, sometimes the memories are so loud I can't escape them. Tonight is one of those nights, and I know I won't be able to sleep. Not with these walls closing in on me.

Grabbing a pillow and a blanket, I take it to my balcony, lying down on the outdoor couch I bought the moment I moved into this place. Out here I can see the nighttime sky, the stars twinkling in the inky blackness, I can breathe without the trapped feeling, and finally I hear what I've craved my entire life.

Peace and quiet.

SEVEN

Kelsea

It's been a full seven days since the last time I saw Nick. He hasn't answered my messages, but I keep sending them, because I want him to know someone cares about him. It's not in me to give up on someone, so I keep trying. Trying to chisel away at the rough exterior around his heart, hoping he'll let me in. All it takes is one fracture, I'll seep in, warm him, show him what a life would be like with the two of us together. It wouldn't always be perfect, but every day Nick would know someone loves him. Someone would wait for him to come home every night.

K: I hope you're having a good day. Not stalking or anything, but I know you're working days this week. Maybe we could see each other one night? I miss my friend, more than anything, Nick. I miss my friend. Please tell me we didn't screw up what we had together. Please.

Tears pool behind my eyes, I hate being that vulnerable with him. It always feels like I'm the only one being vulnerable, but I know if I were to talk to my mom about it, she would say it didn't matter who was vulnerable. Only that someone was. She would tell me laying your soul out there, is the only way to truly fall in love with a person.

I see it, I see the way she and my dad are. The way Ruby and Caleb are. My mom and Ruby are two of the strongest women I know. Every day they send their husbands into a world that isn't safe.

Then the selfish side of me says I'm sending the love of my life out there too, only I won't be the first one notified when shit goes south, because he refuses to accept my feelings.

The stoplight I'm at turns green, so I set my phone down in the cupholder, driving to Ransom and Stella's house. They got back last night, and I'm hoping I won't see Nick, but praying that if I do, it won't be awkward. Turning onto the street, I see her car in the driveway and legitimately almost cry. I've missed her, needed her, and more than anything I want my best friend to tell me it's all going to be okay.

I park quickly and get out, almost running to the door. "Back here, Kels." I hear her, glancing over their privacy fence, grinning when Rambo barks.

Ransom holds the gate open for me, before I give him a fierce hug. "I missed you two."

"We missed you too." He lets me go and I run to my friend, throwing my arms around her. Before I realize it, tears are streaming down my face, and I'm sobbing like a child.

"Kels." She tries to pull my face away from her, but I'm resisting, I don't want either of them to see me like this. At the same time, I can't seem to stop. She's the sister I always wanted, the one person I can let my guard down with. She may judge me but she will never lie to me "Kels, what's wrong?"

For long minutes I just cry, let everything out, trying to purge myself of what I've been feeling the past week. When I pull back, I'm still shuddering, hiccupping, and trying to calm myself down. Ransom has disappeared, leaving just me, Rambo, and Stelle on the back deck. Rambo is always sensitive to how people feel, so when I have a seat on the outdoor couch, he climbs up beside me, putting his head in my lap.

"Sorry." I wipe at my cheeks with the back of my hand, breathing out a gulp of air. "I'm a mess, and I've been a mess for the last few days."

My phone makes a noise in the pocket of my scrubs. Fishing it out, I see a message from Nick, laughing crazily when I read it. The words I've wanted for the last week.

N: I miss you too. Tomorrow night?

Against my better judgment, I text him back.

K: Yeah, tomorrow night.

Throwing my phone down, I put my head in my hands.

"What the fuck happened in the seven days I was gone?" Stelle gives me a look. The look is part worried, part I'm going to call an ambulance if you don't get your shit together and let me know what's going on. "I told you to text me if you needed me. There weren't any texts from you, so I assumed everything was okay."

"I didn't wanna bother you," I start, irritated with myself. "You just found out you're pregnant and on your honeymoon."

"But I'm never too busy for you, Kels. Tell me." Her tone is already that a mother would use when pissed at a kid. She's going to be an amazing parent.

She has a seat on their outdoor couch, patting the cushion next to her. What I wouldn't give for a beer right now, but that's what got me in trouble before.

"Nick took me home from your wedding, because I was too drunk to drive myself after helping you out. When we got there, he and I slept together. More than once." It all comes out in a rush. I worry if I say it slower I won't be able to get all the words out, and I only want to do this once.

Her mouth opens wide, she looks at me, at the ground then back at me, before she squeals loudly.

"Holy shit, Kels! OH. MY. GOD. You slept together?!"

Blowing out a breath, I nod in confirmation. "Twice, and when he left, I texted asking if we could get together. He said we'd talk about it, then he had a horrible call that evening. I heard about it from Caleb. Since then, it's been crickets with Nick. But he just texted saying maybe we could get together this week."

"My brother did that to you?" She levels me with a glare. I know what that means, she's going to give him a piece of her mind, and while I appreciate it, I don't need her fighting my battles.

"I don't need you to be crazy sister right now, I need you to be my friend, Stella."

She reaches out, grabbing my hand. "I'm always your friend, but I'm super pissed at him. Do we have any idea what the call was about?"

Pushing my hair back I do my best to compose myself before I drop the bomb on her. "Child welfare check, and apparently they took the child out of the home."

"Shit." She clucks her tongue. "I wanna be so angry with him, but both of us know what that means."

"I know," I commiserate with her. "Like I'm irritated that he's ignored me, and make no mistake, he has ignored me, but at the same time I kinda get it."

Stella puts her feet on the coffee table in front of her. "I get it too," she whispers. "Still doesn't make it right. I wonder how he's been sleeping. It's calls and situations like that – they push him back three or four steps and then he has to recover those steps. Sometimes it can take days, sometimes it's months. Which I know doesn't help you right now, but I'm telling you this because I don't want you to think it's you. It's not. It's him."

Putting my feet next to hers, I shrug. "I know it's not me, but it hurts the same. And I have no idea. I've thought about surprising him, ya know, just showing up, but we both know that's not a good idea with him."

"He and Ransom are having lunch tomorrow, maybe I should make my baby daddy ask him what the fuck his problem is."

"No." I shake my head quickly, trying to diffuse the situation. "Please don't get in the middle of this. I'm a grown woman, I knew what I was doing when I invited him to my bed, I just didn't think he would ignore me." I tilt my head, the tears coming again. "And I'm fuckin' pissed that I keep crying about it."

"Did anything else happen?" she asks, resting her hands on her slightly bigger stomach. "I gained four pounds, we fucked like rabbits, and lounged on the beach. My husband is hot as hell in a pair of swim trunks with an ocean behind him." She winks. "But we missed Rambo, our bed, and I missed having dinner with you at least three times a week." She rests her head on my shoulder.

"Nick and I used condoms since I'm not on birth control, and the second time we had sex, it broke" My voice is soft. "We got caught up in the moment, and we knew it broke, but we didn't stop."

"Oh Kels, was it a bad time of the month? Could you be pregnant?"

"You know I'm not really regular." My voice is small as I speak to her. "Because of the thyroid issues I have, even with the medication I'm on, and there's never been a reason for me to seriously be on birth control. I've never been in that kind of a relationship, I didn't even realize it broke at first," I admit to her. "All I knew was that it felt good. Different, but good." My face is warm as I tell my best friend everything that happened. "I've never had unprotected sex before. When I felt the warmth against my thighs, I knew the condom had broken. Then Nick said it had, and I didn't know what to say."

"Whatever happens, you know I'll be here for you, right?"

"I know." I give her a sad smile. "I went to work and got Plan B the next day. But there's a small part of me that kinda wished for something more," I admit as I let the tears fall again. "That said, even if that were the only way I could have a piece of him, I'd take it. I know that's sad, and I'm a dumbass for saying it. But I see so much potential in Nick, I just wish he could see it in himself."

Stella hugs me again, running her hand down my arm. "We all do, Kels. We all wish he could see it."

Pulling it together, I turn on the couch to face her. "Enough about me, tell me all about Hawaii."

Her eyes take on a faraway, dreamy look. "The lanai of our hotel room will always hold a special place in my heart," she giggles, and it warms me to my soul to have my best friend back again.

EIGHT

Nick

It's raining slightly as I pull my patrol car up to The Café. I've signaled into dispatch I'm taking a lunch break, and I let my shoulders drop. Since that night with Kels I've been tightly wound.

Not because of what we did together, but because of the way she made me feel. I've always wanted what everyone has. I just convinced myself it would never happen for me. Now? Now I'm not so sure.

Getting out, I lock my patrol car and head into what most of us around town call our home away from home. Caleb proposed to Ruby here, from what I heard Ace and Violet met here, and Ransom's family practically lives here.

I see him sitting at one of the side tables, Rambo at his feet. When he sees me, his tail wags, and I can't help but smile down at the dog. He can always bring a smile to anyone's face. Doesn't seem to matter what they're going through.

"Hey." Ransom reaches out a hand to me when I get close enough. "Good to see you."

"You too." We give each other the kind of bro half-hug you see in every movie. "You're tan." I give him a little shit as I settle in across from him.

"That's what happens when you lay out naked on your private lanai in Hawaii." He gives me a huge grin. "Ordered for you by the way. Barbecue from Smokers is the special."

My damn stomach growls as I think about the little BBQ place that opened up a few streets over from here a few months ago. "Damn, I love when they share business. Their pulled pork with your mom's sides is some of the best food I've ever had."

He laughs. "I know, Stelle's gonna be pissed if she finds out we're having it. She's been craving BBQ for two weeks now."

"Have you all told the parents yet? I have a feeling Mom knows I'm hiding something, so I've avoided going home. She can smell a story at twenty paces."

"We haven't told them yet, but soon we will. We just want to make sure we get through the ultrasound at the end of the week."

I look at my friend, he's glowing. But it's not just with the tan he got on vacation; it's not because he's well-rested from not working, he's happy. I wonder if I've ever looked as happy as he does right now. Before I can stop myself, I ask, "Are you happy?"

His eyebrows narrow together in question, before he speaks. "Happiest I've ever been in my life. Why? Do I not look like I am?"

A waitress brings some drinks and I take a long chug of water. "No, you do, you look the happiest I've ever seen you. It's just..."

"C'mon Nick, spit it out, we're brothers. We can be honest with each other.

I avert my gaze from his eyes, start messing with the wrapped silverware and let the question fly. "Do I look happy to you?"

He pulls back like the words were a slap to the face. Then he looks at me, really looks at me. At the same time I wonder what he's thinking, what he sees, but then I don't want to know either. What if he reads something I don't want to know?

"Honestly? I think you're content, but I wouldn't call you happy. I think you walk around with a smile on your face because that's what you feel you're supposed to do. Happy, though? No."

My fingers play with the straw wrapper, avoiding his eyes as I process the information he gave me. "I'm not," I push out between dry lips. The sound is harsh, like I haven't spoken in years. But it's there. "I'm not happy."

"There." Ransom grins. "You admitted it. Now what are you going to do about it?"

"Make myself happy?"

I have to be some kind of fucking damaged not to know how to be happy.

"You're asking like it's a question as to whether you deserve it or not, Nick. You deserve it. A lot of people struggle with this shit."

"Do they?" I pin him down with my glare. "Do they really? Because to someone like me walking around Laurel Springs is like walking around Happy Town, USA."

"Now you're just being dramatic." He flicks his straw wrapper at me.

"Fuck you, I'm being serious."

"Okay." He leans forward, hand wrapped around his water glass. "What brought this shit on?" He tips the glass to take a drink.

Again my eyes go anywhere but to his face. "Kels and I, we slept together."

And that's when he began to choke to death in the middle of The Café.

RANSOM IS BREATHING NORMALLY AGAIN when we resume our conversation.

"You and Kels slept together? When?"

"The night of your wedding."

"Jesus Christ, Nick. What the hell?"

Normally I don't reveal my feelings about anything, but I know I have to in this situation. "I just got so sick of saying no. I've wanted her for years."

"Then why aren't you with her right now?"

"It's complicated."

He shakes his head as he takes a bite of the food that's been delivered to us. "Bullshit. That's your excuse."

"Excuse?" I'm slightly offended by what he's implying.

"Yeah, don't forget I know you. You don't have to care as long as you don't get too close. If you keep people at arm's length you don't have to show emotion. It's always what you use for your excuse."

"I think I'd prefer calling it a coping mechanism." I take a drink of my water.

He glares. "It's an excuse if I've ever seen one. Nobody is denying you had a shitty childhood, but you can overcome that. You have overcome it."

"But have I? Have I really?"

He shrugs. "Only you can answer that question, Nick. You know yourself better than anybody."

I do know the answer, and that's the bitch of the whole situation. I haven't overcome it. Sometimes I'm not sure if I ever will.

Kelsea

I'm nervous as I drive my Jeep down the dirt road leading to the picnic area where Nick asked me to meet him. It's the original spring, where Laurel Springs got its name from. For years it had been dry, but after the flooding rain we had last year, it's flowing again and cool on these almost muggy nights as we head into summer.

Glancing at the clock on my dash, I see I'm early, but I'm not surprised to already see Nick waiting on me. He's sitting on the tailgate of his truck, looking like the hot, southern boy he is.

Parking, I allow myself to take a few moments longer than I need to, just to look at him. He's hot as hell with no clothes on, but there's something even sexier about him when he wears them. Old, well-loved jeans lay against strong legs, hanging off the tailgate, the threads kissing a pair of scuffed boots covering his feet. My gaze wanders up, seeing threadbare holes where the soft material cups his thighs. They're stained, just on the other side of looking dirty, his torso covered by an old band t-shirt, the arm holes hugely cut out showing his cut abdomen. His five-o-clock shadow darkens his face, a hat pulled low over his eyes hides his gaze from me. In the low-light of the evening, I really wish I could see those eyes of his.

Putting the Jeep in park, I slowly turn it off before getting out. I can feel the gaze following me as I walk over to where he sits.

"Hey girl, hey," I joke, making him laugh.

"Hey," he answers back. "Thanks for meeting me."

I come to a stop in front of him. "Thanks for finally

answering my text. I was beginning to wonder if you were dead."

He drops his head lower. "I deserve that."

"And so much more." It's important to me to show him he can't just keep coming into my life when he wants and then walk out when it gets to be too much for him.

"I've been an asshole." He grins as he reaches out for me.

Our hands touch and I feel it. The awareness I've always had when he's around, the fluttering deep in my stomach, that clench in your gut as you drive over a hill way too fast. I'm holding onto the 'oh shit' handle, praying desperately I don't lose my seat. Nick Kepler though, he'd be worth losing it for.

Without prompting, he moves those hands of his down my arms, my sides, and cups them under my ass before lifting me up onto the tailgate so that I'm straddling his lap. Reaching up, I pull the hat of his head, turning it around to the back, before I place it back where it was.

The two of us are quiet, a symphony of crickets, birds, and the running water, the only soundtrack to this moment in the history of our relationship. He swallows roughly as he flexes his fingers against my ass, pulling me even tighter against him. I watch, fascinated as his Adam's apple moves. Without thought, I lean forward, kissing him softly against the skin of his throat. He moans, a noise deep in his chest.

"What happened?" I whisper, not wanting to break the spell we seem to have wrapped ourselves in. "Why haven't you answered me?"

His hands grip me tighter. "I don't know how to do this, Kels."

"Do what?"

"Be the man you want me to be. The man you deserve. I'm a selfish asshole most of the time." He stops, biting his bottom lip. "I'll probably end up pushing you away and making you hate me."

My heart cracks, I know what he's saying is coming from a genuine place. He wants to protect me. Wants to make sure I know what I'm getting into. "Why don't you let me be the judge of what I can handle, and what I want. I'm stronger than I look."

"It would kill me if I hurt you, like really hurt you."

"You did," I remind him. "When you ignored me for a full week.

"I wasn't ignoring you," he protests. "I just didn't know what to do, how to do this." He motions in between us.

"You have a great example with your parents, Nick, and it's not like I'm an expert. I've only had like two boyfriends my entire life. None of them were you though, I always held them up to what I anticipated you would be." Now is the time to admit things and start fresh.

"I hated both of them," he growls. "No matter who you've been with I've always hated them. I couldn't face being with you, but I didn't want anyone else to have you."

"You really are an asshole," I giggle.

"I won't change overnight," he warns.

"Rome wasn't built in a day, Nick. We'll go slow."

"A date?" he asks. "Tomorrow? I don't work tomorrow."

"I work the morning shift, but I'm free for the afternoon and evening. Whenever you want to go, I'm good."

He leans in, tilting his head. I wait for the kiss, my eyelids flickering shut. When our lips meet, I throw my arms around his neck, digging my fingers in the little bit of hair that hangs below the hat. "Tomorrow afternoon, I'll pick you up at two." His voice is deeper, his eyes darker, and in between where I'm straddling his lap, I can feel his length making itself known.

"Tomorrow," I parrot back. "Two."

He laughs, it's a deep purr. I want to curl myself around his body and hold him tight. "As long as that's okay with you."

"Perfect, what should I wear?"

"Anything you wear you look amazing in, but in this instance wear something you can get dirty."

I raise my eyebrows at him. "How dirty?"

His voice is that dark, deep tone again. Making my toes curl as he answers. "Very, very dirty."

Hugging him close, my mind goes to places it's never allowed itself to go with Nick, and damned if I'm not more excited than I've ever been.

NINE

Kelsea

"Today has been a day."

I turn my head to the voice of my fellow medical assistant, Karsyn. We both started working here at the same time as Stelle, but while she's moved on, we've been holding it down together. She's become one of my closest friends, right next to Stelle.

"Has it been?" I haven't really noticed because all I can think about is Nick picking me up this afternoon.

"Yeah," she sighs. "But that could just be me." She purses her lips. "I've been seeing Tucker off and on for the last few months, more of a friends with benefits thing. I want more, but he's scared. He wants more, but I'm scared. That's how we've been, and now I just don't know what we are."

Tucker, I know that name from somewhere. "How do I know him?"

She gives me a look of surprise, drawing her eyebrows together. "Tucker, you know, the K-9 trainer?"

"Oh right, I'm sorry it's not working out the way you want it to."

The breath she exhales rustles the bangs lying against her forehead. When she looks at me, there's a sadness in her eyes I've never seen before. "Yeah me too, but you never know what tomorrow holds."

Her pain is my pain, I know where she is at this point in her life. Reaching over, I give her a hug, wrapping my arms tightly around her. "I'm sorry, Karsyn."

She pulls back, rubbing her fingertips under her eyes, sniffling. "I'm not sorry for the time we spent together, it was magical. But this?" She blows out a watery breath. "This sucks. Promise me you'll be careful with Nick. He and Tucker, they're a lot alike."

Those words hit me harder than I expect them to. "I promise. I won't get so far in, I can't get out." But I wonder if I'm not already there.

MY HANDS SHAKE as I curl my hair, watching as it bounces against my shoulder. In the mirror I smile at myself, liking the fact I'm fixing my hair for Nick. On the bathroom counter, my phone vibrates. A smiling picture of my mom shows on the screen, asking to FaceTime. Knowing she'll keep calling me until I talk to her, I answer, propping my phone up against the shelving unit on the wall.

"Hey," I answer, giving her a grin.

"Getting ready to go somewhere?"

Holding another lock of my hair up, I curl it around the barrel of the iron before giving her my attention. "Yup, I have a date!"

"Ohh, who with?" If there's one thing Karina Harrison likes, it's to be kept apprised with what her kids are doing.

"I'd rather not say just yet, it's new."

She gives me a look that makes me nervous. "New as in you just met him, or new as in you've known him a while and the relationship part is new?"

"Mooomm." There's a warning to my tone. "Seriously, if it turns into anything you'll be the first to know."

"The hell I will. You'll tell Stella first, then Ruby, I'll be an afterthought."

I laugh at her dramatics. "You're never an afterthought.

"Pretty soon none of you will need me."

"Mom," I reprimand her. "As soon as there's something to tell you, I promise you will know."

"Okay, Kels, I just wanted to call and see what you were up to. I'll let you to go, since you already have plans."

"Love you, Mom. I'll be there for Sunday dinner this week."

She grins brightly. She loves Sunday dinner. "See you then. Love you, Kels."

Turning the phone off, I wonder how long I'm going to be able to stall her. There's only so long Karina Harrison will wait when she smells some gossip. Glancing at the clock, I see I'm running out of time. Hurrying to my closet, I throw the door open.

"Wear something you can get dirty," I remind myself of what he said.

Grabbing out an old pair of jeans and a t-shirt I haven't worn since high school, I quickly get dressed, just as there's a knock on my door.

Nick

As I wait for Kels to come to the door, I flick my keys up and then down in my hand. It's a nervous habit I've had for a long time. Since I was young, I've had ticks, and this is one of them. The door opens and my mouth goes as dry as a desert.

"Hey." She's all bright eyes, toothy grin, and someone whose happy to see me.

"Hey." I grin back. Before I can stop them, my arms circle her waist, bringing her in close, dropping a kiss on her forehead.

The motion makes me start for a moment. I've never, in my life, kissed a woman on the forehead. Covering it up, I release her. "You ready?"

"Is this okay?"

My eyes follow her hands as they run down jeans sticking to her like a second-skin, back up to a shirt hugging her curves. "You're perfect."

I mean those words, more than I have before. If anyone has been the problem between us, it's definitely me. Her cheeks turn pink as she ducks her head and averts her gaze. Reaching across I lift her chin up with my finger. "I'm serious."

She nods slowly. "I know you are. You don't say things you don't mean."

It hits me in the chest how well this woman knows me, and how much ammunition she has to break me in half. Shaking the thoughts from my head, I grab her hand. "C'mon, let's go."

"WHERE ARE WE GOING?" she asks, fifteen minutes later as I turn off the main road onto a dirt trail, rutted from the recent rains we've had.

"Remember when Leigh wasn't sure if she wanted to sell her family property or not? Ransom and I bought some acreage."

This is something not a ton of people know about, we didn't advertise the purchase, because we want the area to be ours and ours alone.

"You did?" The surprise is evident in her voice.

"Yeah, I'm going to get me a building to do my woodworking in, and we're going to put a gym out here so we can all work out as a team," I explain.

"Who taught you how to do the woodwork?"

This subject is another one I haven't spoken about to many. "My dad," I laugh. "When I first came to live with them, I had a really hard time sleeping at night. For a few weeks, I would roam the house, just looking for something to do. One night I was doing it when he came home from work. He took me out to his shop and showed me a few things. Within six months I was selling stuff at the local craft shows, and I took commissions here and there. In this apartment I have, I don't have a place to do it." I shrug.

"I'm sure you could go to your parents'."

"Yeah, go to a cop's house in the middle of the night?"

She gives me a look. "Yeah, that's probably not the best idea." She hangs onto the handle as we go over a particularly deep rut. "So does that mean you aren't sleeping at night?"

"Some nights are better than others." I blow off the question.

There's slight tension in the cab of the truck, I know she wants to ask me exactly what that means, but she doesn't. Pulling up to a locked gate, I turn the truck off.

"From here, we gotta ride." I nod toward an ATV. "You up for it?"

"I'm up for anything with you."

This woman, how much she trusts me, almost kills me. I don't think I've ever trusted anyone in my life as much as she trusts me. I'm not stupid either, I know I don't deserve it.

"NICK, NO!" she screams, laughing as drive us through a puddle, causing mud and water to splash on us.

I laugh along with her. Turning my head back so she can hear me, I yell, "You like it, otherwise you wouldn't be laughing."

"I do." She tightens her arms around my waist, holding on as I take us through another mudhole.

"It's right up here." I point to where two buildings are starting to take shape.

We're quiet as we approach the location, turning the ATV off when we get close enough. "This is where it's going to be." I nod toward the building that will be my shop. "After we get the road laid out here, I'm going to have this row of trees cut." I point to the ones I'm talking about. "With the tress cut, there's a view of pond."

"Any fish in the pond?" She giggles and I do nothing but groan.

"I'm never going to live down that one time I tried to go fishing with y'all." I run my hand over my face. "I think I lost your dad's respect that day."

"Well I knew how to hook a worm and you had no idea. He did kind of question your man card."

"My man card is fully intact," I argue.

Her eyes run up and down my body. There's an awareness stretching tightly between us.

"It seems to be fully intact to me," she agrees.

The wind has kicked up, and I'm noticing the sky darkening. "Looks like it might rain." I hold my hand out to her.

"I don't mind the rain."

Pulling her to me, I push one hand into her hair, wrap the

other one around her waist. "Of course you don't. You have all these romantic notions, Kels. I wish I could be like you."

She twines her arms around my neck, getting all up in my personal space. "I can teach you to be like me." She drops her lips onto mine.

The kiss is soft, slow, sensual, everything that is Kelsea. When we break apart, those eyes of hers are bright as hell again. "What's the most romantic thing you can imagine?" I whisper. Lord knows why I ask her this, I'll never be the type of man who can give it to her.

"A proposal in the pouring rain." She's quick to answer. "I've always thought of the rain as romantic." She bites her lip. "You know, lazy days in bed, wet kisses, soaked clothes."

Listening to her explain why she loves rainy days is almost enough to have me hard. "Maybe I can start looking at rainy days differently."

She leans in, kissing me lightly. "Maybe you can, Nick. Any of us can change, it just depends on how bad we want it."

She's right, and although I want to change, something tells me it won't be that easy. Not letting go of her hand, I walk us over to the ATV. The ride back to the truck is quieter, but not awkward. I find I'm enjoying the little touches Kels sneaks in when we go over a particular bumpy patch of land. The way her breasts rub against my back, makes my dick punch against the zipper of my jeans.

We get back, both getting off, and using two towels I brought with me to clean off before we get back in the truck. The minute we get in, the skies open and the rain pours.

"We made it just in time." I turn us around, heading back toward the main road. "Are you ready for part two?"

"There's a part two?"

"There's always a part two." I reach over, grabbing her hand with mine. "One thing I've learned is there's always a second-chance, always something waiting right around the corner. Are you ready for what's waiting around the corner?"

"If you're there," – she lifts our clasped fingers – "then I'm always ready for what's waiting on me."

TEN

Nick

In the background, I can hear the rush of water, indicating Kels is in my shower. Leaning against the counter in my kitchen, I take a deep breath, trying to calm the heart that feels like it's beating out of my chest. Bringing her here was a conscious decision, having her in my personal space is a way to show her how much I care for her, rather than telling her. I've never been good with words. Hopefully my actions can say what I can't. It had taken me years to tell my mom and dad not only thank you for saving my life, but that I love them. It was a word I felt I couldn't pronounce, no one had ever really said it much to me. Until I came to live with the Keplers. That isn't a time in my life I want to relive tonight.

Moving over to the sink, I look out the window, watching as the rain falls steadily. Sharp bursts of thunder echo every now and again, the loud clap rolling with a deep groan, shaking my apartment building with its ferocity. When I was young, right when the Keplers took me, thunderstorms were my favorite.

Watching and listening to them let me know I wasn't the only thing in the universe with a barely leashed anger. They let me know that humans and objects have a breaking point. Realizing it was okay to let some of your anger out had been imperative to me as a teenager. Whether anyone wanted to deal with it or not, I was a bomb fixing to explode. Much like I am tonight.

I'm trying to ignore that Kels is naked in my shower, that she's here, in my apartment, and I do well for a few seconds. Almost as soon as it began, it ends, because I feel something. There's a prickling in my neck, along my arms, before I even hear her. Fuck, this girl...

Turning around, I lose my ability to speak.

"It's okay I put this on, right?" Kels as she stands in my kitchen, wearing the t-shirt and sweat pants I left for her in the bathroom. They swallow her whole, but I can't deny she looks good in them, a hundred times better than I ever have. I've never been the type of guy to get all fucked up about a girl wearing his clothes, but goddamn if I don't love the fact my clothes are touching her skin. I have to clear my throat. Twice.

"That's what I left them there for."

We stare at one another for a long time before I open my mouth and let words come out again. "I think they look better on you."

She blushes, looking down at the floor as she pushes her wet hair behind her ears. "I've never worn a guy's clothes before. I kinda like it."

"I do too."

In this scenario I want to tell her everything I would like if I had the guts to dream. I'd want her to be mine, want her to go to sleep with me every night and wake up together in the morning. The moment between us gets heavy as we each catch the other's eyes.

"Nick," she whispers. "I'm trying not to scare you off, trying not to take this faster than I should." Her voice trails off.

"I know, I feel it too."

Something I've never felt before. It's almost as if one of us is a magnet, the other a piece of metal. The chemistry between us is palpable. Looking at her across the room is enough to send images of us naked against the sheets of my bed through my head. The thing is, that's not all I want her for. More than anything Kels has been my friend, and I count on her friendship.

Slowly, she walks to me. When she gets close enough, I reach out, hooking my fingers in the waistband of the sweatpants. I pull, she stumbles, landing against my body. Her gaze won't meet mine, and that just won't do for me.

"Look at me, Kels."

Reaching down, I lift her chin with my index finger. We share a breath, our lips barely touching, just enough for me to feel the hint of her body press against mine. Drawing back, I let her eyes take me away, hold me close, and keep me safe from the realities of the life both of us live day in and day out.

"I love those expressive eyes of yours. They say everything your mouth doesn't." My voice is a deep rumble in my chest. "What are you thinking?"

She closes her eyes, tipping her head slightly back. "That I don't want this to end."

I don't either. But I can't say the words aloud. Instead, I tip her chin, capturing her lips with mine. Out of the kisses we've shared, I realize this one is slower, more intimate, and just as important as the rest of them. When we break apart, I give her a smile before reminding her of a normal night between the two of us. "Netflix and pizza?"

The laugh is the one I like the most. Her nose scrunches,

and the smile is infectious. "Only if we can get cheese bread, too."

"I wouldn't dream of not ordering it."

Kelsea

If someone told me three months ago I'd be lying on the couch in Nick's apartment, with his arms around me, I would have said they were crazy. Nothing about this seems like real life to me. Yet, here I am.

Our half-eaten pizza rests on the coffee table, cups with just enough for one more drink sit beside the plates. Any other day I'd be getting up, trying to clean up the mess. I'm not one of those people who can just let a mess stick around. Today, I refuse to move. Nick sleeps against me.

I move just a hair, allowing myself to look behind my shoulder at him. So often when he's awake, he hides his emotions. His face is a brick, immoveable and strong. What I'm finding right now is a softness I've never seen. One phrase I would never use to describe Nick is at peace, but right now, he looks almost peaceful.

This is how every night would be if we were together, I tell myself. I would take care of him, he'd never have to worry about being loved, I'd never have to worry about being too clingy. I almost laugh because he's always warned me that he never sleeps well. Looks like he is right now.

Tucking in closer next to him, I close my eyes, hoping to catch some sleep too. Yawning, I snuggle in, pulling the blanket off the back of the couch around us. As I drift off, I think nothing in the world can be better than what I'm experiencing right here.

THE DREAM WORLD I'm in is dark, I feel something gripping my ribs tightly. I can't breathe and I feel like I'm drowning. Fighting roughly against whatever it is pulling me down. Trying to turn away, something grasps tightly at my neck, squeezing with a force I've never felt before. I'm straining against the dream, finally breaking free. When I reach up there are fingers against my throat, I tug at them, trying to dislodge their grip. I meet resistance and start to panic, trying to scream.

The scream doesn't come out, but I manage to gasp a huge breath in. "Can't..." I fight.

"I can't..." I gouge my nails into the other person's flesh, finally prying enough to be able to move.

"I can't breathe!" Jumping up, it takes me a second to realize where I am and what's happened.

Nick is sitting, staring at his hands.

"What the fuck happened?"

My question is a demand. I've never been in this kind of situation before, and I'm not comfortable being in one now. Both of us stand quickly, looking at one another. The only sound in the room is our labored breathing.

"This." He runs his hands through his hair, his dark eyes tortured as they move up and down my body. "This is why I shouldn't be trusted with you."

I cough loudly, clearing my throat. "No, this is when you're honest with me, and tell me what in the hell this is."

"I'm fucked up." He grips his hair in his fingers, spreading his arms out, trying to get his lungs to expand. "I have nightmares sometimes, but honestly they're more like memories that I can't escape." He turns from me, as I wrap my arms around my body. "Stuff that happened to me when I was younger. I get claustrophobic, half the damn time I sleep outside on the deck, just so I can see the sky. It lets me know nothing can keep me from leaving. I was locked in a closet once," he admits softly.

"Tried to get out and couldn't. I was in there for days, with nothing to eat or drink. Since then, I hate to be in a place where I can't see a way out. It does things to me."

Hearing him say this breaks my heart. I've known him for years, but I never knew this side of him. I've heard our parents whisper, and I've wanted to know, but I never felt like it was my place to come right out and ask.

"Thank you for sharing your past with me." My voice is soft, barely above a whisper. Hoping I don't scare him, I walk closer.

"I could have killed you, and you're thanking me?" He tilts his head back, staring up at the ceiling. "Do you have some sort of death wish, Kels?"

"No, and if I were truly scared of you, I wouldn't still be here."

He walks over to me, leaning down until we're nose to nose with one another. "You should be, I'm scared of myself."

Putting my hand in his, I entwine our fingers together. "I'm willing to help you work through whatever it is you need to work through."

"You're some kinda saint, my own birth parents didn't even want me."

It hurts, knowing how he thinks of himself. "That's on them, Nick, not on you."

"It's all on me, has been my whole life. I've never had anyone to stand behind. It's always been me taking care of myself."`

Those words break me.

"You need to open your eyes, Nick. There's love completely surrounding you from all sides. The Kepler's have loved you since the day they brought you home, even if you didn't want to let them. You and Ransom have been best friends for years. He would do anything for you. Your coworkers, the MTF family. Even Rambo loves you, and we all know that animals are the best judges of character. Don't forget me, I've loved you since I was a kid. I'll stand in front of you, Nick." I'm crying now, tears slipping down my face unchecked. It's messy and ugly, like life.

"Don't cry for me," he whispers, barely hanging onto his emotions.

His eyes are red, wet, his jaw a tight, chiseled line, staring at me like he's never seen me before.

Wiping my face, I put one hand around my stomach, the other to my mouth. My head tells me to hold this shit back, but my heart? My heart knows it has to come out.

"I want to cry for you." I choke out the last word.

"Why?" He's got his hands in his short dark hair, pulling at the roots. "Why won't you just let me go?"

"Like everybody else does?" I finish the statement for him. "Like every other girl you've been in a relationship with? Like your birth mom and dad did? That's what you know, isn't it? That's easier for you."

"Kelsea, stop it."

"No," I continue, this time stepping up to him, pointing at his chest, getting up in his face. "I'm not going anywhere, Nick, you can try to scare me away, but it's about time you learned what it's like for someone to stand in front of you."

He makes a noise of disbelief in his throat, but I don't pay attention.

"I will protect you." I put my hand on his heart. "I will be the person you can always count on. I'll be the one who filters all the shit so you can see all the good. Somebody comes for you? They come through me."

His chest is heaving, his eyes are closed. "I don't deserve it," he pushes between his lips.

Putting my hands on his cheeks I force his head level with mine. "Open your eyes."

It takes him a few moments, but he finally does. "You deserve everything. Just like I do, and we're gonna have it together, Kepler."

"You think so?" He's slightly smiling.

"I know so." I lean forward, kissing him, tasting the salt of my tears and the promise of what I hope is a future.

ELEVEN

Kelsea

N: I'm really sorry about what happened at my apartment. I've never allowed a woman to sleep over, because I was scared of what would happen. When I was a teenager, I would wake up with my hand tight around a pillow. I've never given myself a chance to see what would happen with someone else…until you.

K: I told you, I'm not upset with you, I'm sorry you have those memories and I would do anything to help you get over them, if you would allow me to.

I bite my thumb nail, wondering how he's going to respond to what I've said. With him, I'm not ever sure how he will react.

N: Shrinks don't work with me. Back when I first came to live with my parents, they sent me to a shrink, who put me on some medication. The

medicine took away my feelings totally. I was like a zombie and I hated it.

K: So how did you convince them to take you off of it?

N: I told them I was better, that I hadn't had a nightmare in a long time.

Oh my God, he lied to them, and he's been dealing with this on his own since then!

K: Nick, lying to them wasn't the answer.

N: Get off my case, Kels. It's the only answer I had back then. Do you know what it's like to go from feeling everything to feeling nothing? I didn't want to be angry all the time, but I at least wanted to feel joy.

K: They have new medications now, Nick. Maybe there's a new one out there that will give you peace of mind and won't turn you into a zombie. I'm willing to help you find it.

N: You're too good for me.

I blush from those words. They're the closest he's ever come to saying he truly cares about me. I'll take what I can get, but I want him to understand his worth.

K: No Nick, I'm what you deserve.

When he says nothing else, I give myself a pat on the back. at least he didn't argue with me.

IT'S BEEN three days since I've seen Nick. Not that I haven't tried to see him, especially after the way we left each other, which was brutal. It just hasn't worked out. He hasn't completely ghosted me, we've texted a few times here and there, but it's not the same as hearing his voice, seeing his face. I'm kind of sad, as I glance at my cell phone, wishing for a message from him. I'm living for them these days.

Sighing, I go back to work, looking up when I see Karsyn walking over.

"Can you take the next one?" Karsyn asks as I sit at the registration desk, filling out notes for the last patient I had. "Tucker's stopping by," she says softly.

"Aww, K, are you gonna be good?" I can already tell she's trying to hold it together, and after my night with Nick, I'm feeling closer to her. I understand her more than I ever have. Both of us seem to have the pleasure of loving men who don't think they deserve to be.

She nods almost stoically. "Yeah, I have to be." She comes behind the desk, grabbing a bag. "His stuff." The look on her face kills me.

"Take your time, I'll cover for you."

As I watch her back, I wonder if one day this will be me. Loving a man who can never fully love me back and being heartbroken when it's over. The thought makes me sad, but at the same time, I think I'd rather have one day of pure happiness than a lifetime of never having my heart speed up at the sight of the person who holds it in the palm of their hand.

Pulling up our scheduling software, I write down the next patient's name on an empty chart before going to the waiting room. "Metcalfe," I call out, surprised when I see Roselynn, a school social worker we've worked with before, stand up with a young boy. I play it off, steeling my gaze. "Right this way. Let's get you weighed and then we'll get you into an exam room."

Weighing him, I check his age on the sign in I printed. he's thin for ten years old, almost on the malnourished side. I'll be sure and say something to the doctor before he goes in. "If you'll follow me, we'll get you set up."

I show the boy the room he's going in, giving him a soft smile. The social worker stays behind. "Depending on what the doctor finds, I may have to call the police," she whispers. "Also, I need a witness, can you be in here when the doctor is?"

"No problem, let me go get him and fill him in on what's happening. We'll be with you two as soon as possible."

My legs shake as I take the hallway quicker than I normally would. There's a rumbling in my stomach, an uneasiness I've never felt before. Granted, I've had cases that broke my heart, but something about the boy reminds me of Nick.

"Dr. Patterson, there's a potential problem in exam room three."

He gives me a concerned glance. "What's going on?"

Briefly I give him the rundown.

"Alright." he nods. "Let's go in, no point in keeping this boy waiting."

I DON'T SAY anything as I watch Dr. Patterson do his examination. I sit back, listen and make notes, knowing they will be imperative for later on. When the doctor has him take some deep breaths, I make note that it appears more difficult than what should be usual for him.

"Darren, is that difficult?" He softly questions.

"To breathe? A little."

"What hurts?"

I watch as he points to his ribcage. When Dr. Patterson starts feeling and slightly manipulating the bones and skin, I can see anger in his eyes. "Okay, Bud, I'm gonna need you to take your shirt off so I can see what I'm feeling better."

Darren acts like he doesn't want to, looking at the social worker for approval. When she gives it, he slowly lifts his shirt.

Holding back my gasp is the hardest thing I have ever done. There are bruises in different stages of healing all along his skin. Some look older, others look brand new. Dr. Patterson asks a few more questions, but truth be told, I don't hear them. All I can do is look at this poor child and wonder who in the hell would want to hurt him.

I ask that question of the social worker as they finish up. She's asked me to come outside to fill out some paperwork.

"His father was arrested a few days ago, but he made bail. It looks like Darren slipped through the cracks. He was given to his aunt, but when his father came to get him, he was allowed to leave. He came to school today complaining of pain in his side. The teachers suspect his home situation IS volatile, which is why I was called in," she explains as she runs a hand across her forehead.

"So what happens now?" I'm almost scared to ask the question. It doesn't seem like it could get worse for Darren, but I have no idea how this process works. In the time I've worked here we've only been involved in a few cases like this.

"Now we call the police and make a statement."

The words make me sick to my stomach. "Will he be removed from the home? I'm sorry if I'm prying, but this breaks my heart."

"No, I completely understand. He will be removed from the home this time and placed into foster care since the aunt is the next of kin and we've already established she can't be trusted. We'll move to have him entered into the system."

She says it so matter-of-factly. And I guess it is. This is something she does every day. She breaks up families because doing so protects one of the parties. "Do you have any idea what kind of a home he'll be placed in?"

"There are foster families in the area, and we also have a group home."

When she says group home, my stomach drops. It literally falls to the floor as I think of Darren – the small kid who looks six or seven, but is really ten – in a group home. I wonder if anyone will care what his favorite toy is, what movies he likes to watch, what are his tv shows, does he have a favorite shirt he likes to wear? Will he get to bring his favorite shirt with him?

I don't realize I've asked the questions aloud until the social worker answers.

"He won't go home to get his things, no. When he's placed, the foster parents will be provided a stipend to get him started in his new home."

I nod, like I understand, but I don't understand at all. How parents can do this to their children, how children who have to go through this become adults in this crazy world. It's then I think of Nick. They become adults because they have to, and sometimes the road to becoming an adult leaves scars that don't seem to go away.

"I HEARD THEY CALLED THE PD," Karsyn says as I make my back to the registration desk. I've been tasked with looking up Darren's medical records to see if he's ever been brought in for something like this before.

"Yeah, he's really bad," I confirm, grabbing an empty computer and getting to work on it. "How did it go with Tucker?" Hopefully talking with her about normal stuff will keep my mind off the million things I have running through it.

"It was brutal," she sighs. "Neither one of us really want to break up, but we can't seem to figure out how to be together." She shrugs. "I don't know. It was the best nine months of my life. I've never fallen like that for a guy before, and when I fell I went all in. To say I'm heartbroken is an understatement."

I see so much of myself in Karsyn right now. She loves a man who can't outrun his past. "Do you regret it?"

She faces me with a sad grin. "Not at all. I've waited my whole life to feel the intensity and passion with a man like I felt with him. Maybe I'm stupid, but I haven't ever been with someone I just had to see every day. Anytime we were alone, I couldn't keep my hands off him. I'll never give up those memories." She sighs. "Like I said, maybe I'm stupid, but at least I can say I experienced an all-consuming love. It's more than many can."

"You're right, most people can't say they have."

She gets up, comes over to me and bends down, hugging me tightly around the shoulders. "I can tell why you're asking, and I can tell you, you won't regret giving Nick a chance."

A laugh breaks its way out of my throat. "What if he isn't willing to give me a chance. It's kind of the other way around."

Her pretty blue eyes sparkle as she looks down at me. I'm not sure if it's with sadness or mischief. "Then make him an offer he can't refuse, Kels."

"I'm pretty sure Nickolas Kepler can refuse anything and everything," I groan. "There's never been a martyr like him."

"Oh, there's something, I promise there will be something. And when there is, make the offer and see what happens."

As she leaves I think hard about what she's said. If we're meant to be together, we will be – that's what happened to everyone else in my family. I trust fate, it's never steered us wrong before.

TWELVE

Nick

I'm just about to clock out for my shift when a call comes over the radio, advising us of a disturbance at the Urgent Clinic. My adrenaline spikes because I know that's where Kels is. It worries me since we've been texting most of the day, but she didn't describe a disturbance.

"Dispatch, show me as responding."

Flipping the lights and shoving my foot against the pedal, I feel the acceleration, gripping the steering wheel tight. If there's one thing I appreciate about my job, it's the ability and permission to drive just on this side of out of control. Approaching an intersection, I slow, checking to make sure I'm seen, before driving through it. "Three minutes out," I inform dispatch.

"Right behind you." I hear Ransom's voice come over the radio.

Hearing him gives me a feeling of safety, knowing my best friend has my back. If I were to ever have a partner on the job, it would be him. The three minutes it takes me to get there feels like years. Ransom pulls up right behind me, we walk in together, but nothing seems out of the ordinary.

Looking around the lobby and front entrance, I see Karsyn, who waves us back.

"What's up?" I ask her as she escorts us into a room.

"Dr. Patterson and Kels will be in here as soon as possible to talk to you. I believe there's also a social worker here."

As she leaves, me and Ransom look at each other. "What the hell is going on?" We both have seats.

"No clue," he answers, stretching out.

"How's Stelle?" I make conversation because I can't stand the quietness of the room.

"Sick, she's having all-day sickness. We're just crossing our fingers that when she makes it to the second trimester she'll be better. Some days she's good, other days she's puking all day long. I don't know how she handles it. She's tired, though, all the time."

"Yeah, I tried calling her the other day, but it went to voicemail." I play with a piece of paper on the table. "Newsflash, she didn't call me back." I pretend to be hurt.

"You got shit to take up with your sister, take it up with her, don't be tattle telling on her with me. I already got a minefield called pregnancy hormones to walk delicately through." He shakes his head, giving me the finger.

"Poor thing," I placate him.

"Fuck you, this shit is hard. She got mad at me the other day because I chose to have one mother fuckin' sushi roll. She can't have sushi. To 'pay me back' her dinner was cookies. Like that bothers me." He breathes heavily. "All I did was tell her it's probably not the best idea for her and the baby, then all hell broke loose."

I laugh hard, putting my hand on my stomach. "What did

she do?"

"Went to your goddamn parents' house for dinner. I had a lengthy text conversation with Ryan." He rolls his eyes.

"Oh I bet you did, messing with his baby girl like that."

"Baby girl, my ass. She's a T-Rex when she gets mad."

"I don't feel sorry for you."

"I don't need you to feel sorry for me, I feel sorry enough for myself, thank you very much."

Just as I'm about to go back into it with him, the door to the room opens, and in walks Kels, Dr. Patterson, and someone else I don't know. My eyes immediately go to Kels; they look down her scrub covered body, and I can't help but to imagine what she looks like against the sheets of my bed.

I don't like how pale she is though, and again I wonder what the hell is going on.

"Officers, this is Roselynn Honeycomb, she's the social worker who takes care of the schools in Laurel County. She brought a student in today." Dr. Patterson makes the introduction.

Ransom and I shake hands with her, before sit down, and get prepared to take notes. "Why don't you start off by telling us why you actually brought him in, who made the first complaint?"

"His PE teacher," she says slowly. "Apparently he couldn't do everything he was supposed to do, and when the teacher questioned why he couldn't do some of the athletic requirements, he talked about how much it hurt. The teacher got suspicious and asked if he could take a look. When he did, he saw bruising on the abdomen, back, and sides of the child. I was called, and I brought him here."

"What did you find to be the case?" I ask Dr. Patterson, giving him my attention.

"He's got several healing injuries and some that are brand

new. From looking at his records, there's a long history of what I think is child abuse. I pulled his records, and while I can't give those to you without a subpoena, I can tell you, I've treated him for suspicious bruises and cuts before. There is definitely a pattern."

This shit pisses me off to no end. Patterns. I had patterns in my life and nobody had noticed them either. Silently I'd cried out for someone to help me. My eyes had begged for anyone to take notice. For fifteen years I'd suffered at the hands of various boyfriends and one mean stepfather. That all changed the day Ryan Kepler walked into my life, and I haven't looked back.

I am one of the lucky ones. There are thousands who aren't, and I feel for them every day. This child needs a voice, and I promised to make myself a voice that could be heard on the day I became a Kepler.

"Can we meet with him? Ask some questions?"

The social worker speaks up. "As long as I'm there."

"Perfect." I make a note in my book. "Let me know when you're ready and he's available."

"Let me go get him." She excuses herself, going to get the child. Ransom talks to the doctor, asking something about morning sickness. I take the opportunity to speak to Kels.

"How is he, really?" I ask softly.

"He's scared, and he's been conditioned to accept his punishment, I'm afraid. At the very least he has some therapist appointments in his future." She holds herself with her arms, one wrapped up to cup her shoulder, the other one around her waist. "Reminds me a lot of you, to be honest."

I don't take offense to what she's said, but it does break my heart for this kid. No one should grow up the way I had to grow up. We're interrupted as the door opens and I see the kid. Darren notices me immediately, running to me, throwing his arms around my legs.

Surprised, I try to take a step back but he's hanging on for dear life.

"Darren, are you okay?"

When he pulls away, I can see the tears in his eyes. "It happened again."

Fuck if those words don't kill me, if I don't personally feel like this is a slap in the face. It's my job to protect people, and I couldn't protect him. The hardest thing? It's like looking down at a younger version of me.

"I know, I'm sorry. What happened?"

Crouching down, I curl my hand around his neck in what I hope is a soothing gesture. To this day I sometimes make the wrong social moves.

"I don't even know." Those tears roll down his eyes, making tracks against his skin. I remember this, remember not knowing why my mom and stepdad were mad at me. What about me made me so annoying? "I was quiet," he sobs. "Tried my best to fade into the background, not to make noise and not to need anything."

I've done the same thing so many times, and I know this pain. When it fails, you're lost. Lost because this is your last hope. Being ignored is so much better than feeling fists, belts, or even verbal assaults. "I know you did, and regardless of what you said or did, you didn't deserve this."

"What did you do?" he asks, his eyes big as they look into mine. "How did you get away?"

The story I'm about to tell him is truly ironic. "A police officer found me, he and his wife adopted me after I was taken from my mom's care."

"A police officer found you like you found me?"

God how I wish it were that simple. Nothing about this situation is simple, but I also realize I have to be the one person who will be honest with him. "Yeah, and then he adopted me."

"Can you adopt me? I don't want to go home anymore. I hate it there, if they send me back, I'll really run away this time."

His face is getting red as he gets angry. I'm sure living on the streets, not knowing where his next meal will come from is a better alternative, but for me that's not going to work.

Kels steps in when it's obvious I don't have the right words. She bends down until she's at eye level with him.

"Right now I don't know what's going to happen." She speaks slowly and calmly. "But what I can promise you is that we will," – she points to me and then herself – "do our absolute best to get you out of the situation you're in. Does that mean it'll happen overnight? Probably not. There are rules and laws that have to be followed. What I can tell you, and honestly tell you, is that Officer Kepler and I are worried about you, and you only. You're our top priority.

He nods stoically, holding his trembling chin as still as he can. Something tells me he's never been anyone's top priority before. Kelsey and I both look at the social worker. It's almost like a standoff until Dr. Patterson says something about going to get Darren something to eat. As soon as he leaves the room, I feel the tension rise, and I know it's time to forget all the shit that's happened to me in my past. My past wasn't great, but if I could make new memories for someone in my situation. I would damn sure do it.

Kels comes to stand beside me, putting her arm in mine. The two of us make a united front as we face the social worker. She looks like she doesn't want to face off with us, and that's fair. Together Kels and I are unstoppable. Neither one of us take no for an answer when that situation is this important, and we're both stubborn as hell. This woman and Darren's father, have met their match. This won't happen again. Not on our watch.

THIRTEEN

Kelsea

"So what's the plan?" I ask, moving my hand down Nick's arm before grabbing his hand in mine. He's an anchor, keeping me solid when all I want to do is rage at the injustice of all of this. "There has to be a plan." Glancing a look over at him, I can see he looks just about how I feel – like I'm going to throw up right here on the floor. Or maybe scream, just to get the nerves out. This moment is so crucial. A child's life remains in the balance of what happens in this one set of circumstances that probably will end up being a few short seconds of his entire life. I feel the pressure as I take a deep breath, blowing it out slowly, hoping to relieve some of the tension.

"He'll go into foster care," Nick says, his voice monotone, his body tight. "Right?" He barks so harshly that I feel sorry for this woman. "You'll put him in some group home, or with a couple who only take children because they get the kickbacks from the government."

"There are many options..."

"Don't give me that shit." Nick jerks my hand out of his, pushing it through his hair. Pointing his finger at her. "You know there aren't any great options for this kid, just like I do." He looks as if he wants to say more, but he's holding himself back.

"Then what do you suggest she do?" Ransom speaks up from where he's been sitting. "I understand why you don't want him in the system, and I understand where you're coming from, Nick, but that doesn't fix the problem. So what's your solution?"

Nick's dark eyes cut over to his friend. If I were on the receiving end of that stare, I might wilt and die. "I don't know," he admits. "Anything has to be better than what he's been facing."

"You got out of the situation he's in, what was the change for you?" Ransom presses, seeming to think Nick has all the answers. "If they don't have a solution, then it's up to us to make one."

Roselynn looks back and forth between all of us. "How about we sit down and discuss this like the adults we are. All we're doing right now is getting irritated and frustrated. None of that helps Darren's situation."

"She's right." I back her up, pulling out a chair and having a seat. We must all make a defensive picture, everyone trying to fight for this kid, but ending up just getting irritated at one another.

She follows my lead, and as we stare at Nick, he finally relents.

He walks back to his seat, sitting with a huff. His body language conveys that he likes none of this, but there's not much any of us can do. If the answers were easy, this wouldn't be a problem in the first place.

"To answer your question," – he looks at Ransom – "what

got me out of that situation was Ryan and Whitney adopting me. I was lucky enough that they saw me, wanted me, and knew the right people to get it working fast."

"Correct me if I'm wrong, but can the same thing happen for him?" he asks Roselynn.

Her body shifts in the seat, almost as if she's uncomfortable under his gaze. I know I would be. "If extenuating circumstances are presented and the person or people want to take possession of the child, it could be fast tracked."

"Possession of the child?" Nick makes a face. "It's almost like you forget this is a person. It's his life we're talking about here."

"I do understand that." She raises her voice to him. "But you have to understand where I'm coming from, Officer Kepler, my hands are tied half the time."

"So what can untie them?" I ask softly.

"If there is a *couple* who can provide a stable home, then the courts are more willing to fast track. Especially if that couple includes a cop and a medical assistant." She looks at both of us.

"We're not." I gesture between us. "We're not really that kind of a couple yet."

Ransom pipes up. "But you could be, and I know both of you would do this for a child who needed the help."

Nick and I look at one another. Would we really do this to save a child's life? "What would be the requirements?" I can't believe I'm asking this.

"You two have to share a residence with an expectation of marriage, if you aren't already married. The home would need to pass inspection, there's a list of things."

Nick and I look at each other. There's something in his eyes. He can't leave Darren in the same situation he was in, and honestly, I can't let him stay there either. Knowing what he's endured, and most likely will endure... I just can't. "We'll do it," I find myself saying before I can regret it.

"Are you sure?" His dark eyes burn into mine. "There won't be any going back, Kels."

"I'm positive." I nod, glancing over at Roselynn. "Let's get this show on the road."

WITHIN THE LAST TWO HOURS, things have happened in a whirlwind. Nick and I have signed the preliminary papers that will petition the courts to have Darren placed with us as a foster child. A lawyer friend of Dr. Patterson's, Taylor, who looks like she walked straight out of a New York fashion ad, is sitting with the group, pushing some more paperwork that we need to read. Darren has been taken to a group home for the next forty-eight hours to allow us time to get an emergency hearing called.

I watched him as he left; he had hope in his eyes. For the first time, he didn't seem beaten down by the system, or a father who never cared. It's a huge responsibility we're undertaking and I pray Nick and I can handle it.

"I'm not going to sugarcoat this," Taylor says. "From everything I've been able to read, the father will fight. Not because he wants Darren, but because he like to control Darren. The two of you will have to be able to handle him, as well as Darren."

"I've handled men like him my whole life." Nick takes a drink from a bottle of water someone gave us at some point in this long afternoon.

My throat is dry as I try to swallow around the bulge there. This is so much more than either of us thought it would be.

"The expectation of marriage..." she trails off. "We'll need her to wear a ring. It will be imperative for the two of you to live together, have a joint checking account. Whatever happens after it's determined who will have permanent custody of Darren is up to you, but until that point, you'll need to be believable."

Nick and I both voice our understanding as we sign even more paperwork.

"I'll give you this week and the rest of next week off with pay," Dr. Patterson is saying.

"That's way too much." I shake my head.

"It's in the handbook," he interrupts me. "If you have an adoption, then you're eligible for the same kind of leave a woman physically having a baby is as well. After next week, we'll discuss if you need further time off."

"That leaves only Karsyn." I worry my thumbnail.

"We'll make it work, Kelsea. I can get some temp help and search for a new assistant. I never replaced Stella. It's about time."

This whole situation is moving so much quicker than I ever imagined it would. My head is spinning as I try to remember everything Nick and I need to do.

"That's the end of it." Taylor grabs up all the papers, putting them in her briefcase. When I was little, I always thought people who had briefcases were the coolest people ever. In my mind they had jobs that were so important, they needed to carry them around all the time. "My advice to the two of you is go home, get some sleep, and tomorrow will start the fight for Darren's life."

By this time, it's well past closing time. Walking out into the mugginess of the night, I turn to Nick. "I'm assuming we should move into your apartment, because of the balcony." I gently grab his hand.

"That'll be best. I have a two-bedroom. We'll have to share."

Wrapping my arms around his neck, I place a chaste kiss on his lips. "Believe it or not, that won't bother me one bit."

But as I drive away, watching him in my rearview, I wonder if the thought bothers him.

FOURTEEN

Ryan (Renegade)

As soon as I see my son walk through the doors of my shop, I know something's wrong. His shoulders are dejected, his eyes have an anger in them I haven't seen in years. I'm worried, even though I know he's a man now. Hell, he's been a man since he was a teenager. I still worry though, really worry that he'll never be able to overcome the way he was brought into this world.

"Hey, Dad." He waves slightly before turning to shut the door.

"Hey," I answer back, not stopping the crib I'm working on.

"Did Stella and Ransom tell you?" He nods to the piece in front of me.

I can't help the wide smile that spreads across my face. "Yeah, shoulda known they told you first. You and Stella have always had a close relationship."

"We have." He walks over to the refrigerator I keep in here.

Carefully I watch him open the door, pull a beer out, then come sit down on one of the empty benches. He's still in full gear, and no matter how badly I want to press him, I know I shouldn't. We're quiet for what feels like a million years. Him slowly sipping on the bottle, me sanding away at the crib that my grandchild will lay in at night. I'm waiting until they tell me if it's a boy or a girl, then I'll paint it.

Stealing a look at Nick, I wonder when he'll be ready to talk. "You know," I start off in the quietness of the room. "I remember when you first moved in. You'd come out here and watch me work all the time. This had always been such a private thing for me. While your mom and Stella love the things I've made for them, they've never watched me work. At first, I found it disconcerting that you watched me, then I got used to it. When you asked me to teach you to do all this stuff, I was so excited because I had someone else who would love what I love," I grunt out as I turn a screw. "Then when you moved out, it was back to this solitary thing again. I have to admit – I've missed having you out here, watching me."

"It fascinated me," Nick says softly. "To watch you do something with your hands like that. You never forced a board in where it didn't go, never got angry when you measured something wrong, and laughed if the color you painted something was completely wrong. You have to understand, I came from a home where strong hands meant bruises. Then when you started to teach me, I loved you even more, because you showed me what I could do with my frustration. There've been many times, even today when I've taken a frustrating day out on some wood working project."

I turn around to face him. "You always used to come out here, too, because you had a lot on your mind. So why don't you tell me what's happening, and maybe I can help you."

He takes another drink of his bottle before grimacing. "Not real sure you can help me with this, Dad."

"But I can try, and sometimes that's all you need."

He drains the beer, throwing it in the trashcan before he runs his fingers through his hair and starts talking. "There's this little boy, his name is Darren..."

"DO YOU THINK WE'RE STUPID?" He finishes up the story.

I take a long drink of the beer I had to get while he was telling me about this child. "No, I don't think you're stupid, but you may be surprised at how much it will strain a relationship to have a kid in the mix."

"I don't think mine and Kels relationship can get any more strained than it was."

A dark laugh works it's way out of my throat. "You would be surprised. But more than anything, I want you to understand what you're inviting into your home. I know you've dealt with children like this before, and you were a child like this, but it's different when it's in your own home. There may be emotional outbursts, he may need to be reassured more than most, scared you're going to leave and never come back. I'm not going to lie, it's a lot to take on."

He lifts his head, looking straight into my eyes. "But it's worth it, right?"

There's a look there, and I know he's asking me if he was worth it. "I wouldn't trade it for anything. You completed our family, Nick. Who knows, maybe Darren and Kels, they'll complete yours. You're not going to know until you give it a shot."

"What if she doesn't want to deal with all this shit, so early in a relationship?"

"Trust me, if she didn't want to deal with it, she wouldn't have offered to help. Kels cares a lot about you, she always has, you've never wanted to see it," I tell him all the things I've seen over my lifetime.

He gets up, stretching, looking out the window. "It's late, I should go. Thank you for the talk, and I'm sure I'll be asking you and mom so many questions, you'll shut your phone off."

"Not a chance, Nick," I grab him up in a hug, holding on a little tighter than normal. "I'm proud of you. You've got this. You'll make Darren's life better, I know it."

"WAS THAT NICK I SAW?" Whitney asks as she stands over the stove, making dinner.

"It was, you'll never believe what he's doing." I walk over to the sink, putting my hands under the faucet and soaping up.

"Dating Kelsea? It's about time."

A grin spreads across my face. "That's not all he's doing. He's about to make one of the most adult decisions I've ever seen him make."

"Now you're starting to worry me. Adult decisions? What kind of adult decisions and why does he have to make them?"

I have a seat at the breakfast bar. It's funny, I can remember almost every conversation she and I have had when she's been at the stove cooking and I've been sitting here talking to her. We've done this for years, actually I can't even remember a time when we didn't do it anymore. It's like my life is split into two parts before Whitney and after Whitney. I wonder if that's how Nick thinks about us adopting him? There's no way for me to ease into this, so I'm throwing a hail Mary like an Alabama quarterback.

"He's trying to foster a little boy he met on a call."

She stops what she's doing, turning around to look at me with wide eyes. "Are you serious?"

"Wouldn't lie to ya, babe. He's really doing it."

"Well, what do we need to do to help him?"

This woman, the mother of my children, she's always amazed me by how good of a mom she truly is, by how selfless she is when it comes to the two of them. "He didn't ask for help."

She turns off the burner, removing the skillet from the heat, and methodically does the same to whatever's in the oven. With the grace she's always had and the swagger she normally puts in her hips for me, she makes her way across the kitchen, stopping on the opposite side of the bar. "He won't ask for help. It's up to us as his parents to give it to him, whether he asks for it or not."

This is what I love about her. She reads people so well, and she doesn't wait for them to ask, Whitney just does what's right.

"Will they give him a foster as a single man?"

Oh this is going to be fun. "That's where things get a little tricky, too. He's been seeing Kelsea."

"As in cute-as-a-button Kelsea Harrison?"

"The one and only. The social worker who was in on this said they need to live together. He's already got an attorney who will help and they're moving in together tomorrow."

"Wow." She breathes a long breath. "I'm proud of him."

Leaning over, I cup her face in the palm of my hand. "Then you should call him and tell him, cause I'm pretty sure he thinks he's in way over his head. It would do him good to hear his mom tell him he's doing a good thing."

"Be right back, you go ahead and eat." She waves me over to the stove. "I have plans to make with my son."

I'm chuckling as I watch her grab a notebook, pen, and her cell phone. I know one thing is for sure, when she gets done with him, Nick won't know what the hell hit him.

FIFTEEN

Kelsea

"What are you going to do with your apartment?" Dad demands as I sit in the living room telling him about the decision Nick and I have made.

It feels a little like I'm being interrogated by Officer Harrison right now. While I can understand why he's suspicious, it's still uncomfortable for me. I've never been the type of person to make waves.

"We're still in preliminary stages right now, but the plan is for Cutter to take over the lease, and he'll keep the furniture. We'll see what the future holds as far as all of that goes."

I look between my mom and dad as they share a conversation between their eyes. I'm proud to say I've never been the type of kid who did something to embarrass or disappoint them. For the most part I've been a good kid most of my life. I'm beginning to think I'm about to get yelled at.

"Kels." Mom crosses her legs, leaning forward with her elbow on her knee. "Do you think this is a good idea? We all know how you feel about Nick, have known it for years. Do you think you can handle it if the two of you don't work out?"

Hearing my mom voice one of my worst fears is like a punch to the gut. Not because I'm embarrassed about everyone knowing how I feel, but because I have the same fears. Instead of admitting to her she might be right, I have to make a compelling argument she'll believe. "This is about way more than if I think Nick and I can handle a relationship."

"Exactly. There's a child involved. What about his mother?"

My frustration level is at a nineteen. Running my fingers through my hair, I tersely respond. "I don't have all the answers, and you wouldn't either. All we're trying to do is what's best for Darren. A lot of the answers will come in the long run."

My eyes go between them, looking for just a little bit of understanding. When I'm not seeing enough, I decide to delve back into teenage-Kels. "Please, for me? Nick never asks anyone for anything. He's asking for this, and I'd like to give it to him. If it hadn't been for Whitney and Ryan, we wouldn't even know Nick now. He just wants to give back to the system that helped him."

Dad is the first to relent, as I knew he would be. "Okay, if this is truly what you want to know, you know we support you. I just don't want to see you get hurt."

I don't want to see myself get hurt either, but something tells me that I'm not in charge of this journey. Fate, happenstance – whatever this is – has taken hold of our lives and is gonna put us where we're supposed to end up. It's going to spin us around in a circle and let us fall where we may. All we can do is hang on for the ride and hope it doesn't make us so dizzy we won't be able to see straight when it's all over.

"Do you need help getting your clothes over to Nick's?" Dad asks. "I'd like to have a conversation with him."

"Promise me you won't make this awkward."

He chuckles. "Oh Kels, I can't make that promise."

"Well can you promise me when you do have that conversation with him, I'll be out of earshot. Honestly, my soul can't take it."

"Hey." He grabs for my hand, pulling me into a hug.

Right then I'm transported back to all the times my Dad gave me a hug and told me it'd be alright. He's worn the same cologne as far as I can remember, and I fit right under his chin like I always have. Wrapping my arms around him, I squeeze tight.

"What you're doing is the right thing," he encourages me. "I know it may seem like you're heading into the headlights of an oncoming car on a rainy night, when you aren't sure if they're in your lane or not. Raising a child is scary, Kels. One whose obviously been in the situation Darren's been in? Doubly scary. But I'll tell you this, he needs you, and if you're willing to help then you've done more for him in the past couple of days than his parents have done for him his whole life. Of course your mom and I are scared for you. That's our job. You advocate for Darren. We advocate for you."

Pulling away I wipe my eyes and cheeks. There's something about hearing my dad give me a speech that tugs on my heartstrings like nothing else does. To know he's proud of me is the best thing in the world.

"Mom, I do need help packing my car up, but I can take everything over to Nick's, if the offer still stands."

"Of course." She gets up. "Let me go get my purse and call Ruby, you know she's more than willing to help too."

When she leaves, I look at my dad. "Promise me. If you talk to him, it's not while I'm around."

He makes a motion of crossing his heart. "I promise."

Mom comes into the living room. "Ruby's meeting us over there, so we should get going."

Within five minutes, I'm back in my car, heading toward my apartment for possibly the last time, my mom in my rearview. I take a deep breath, feeling the tension release from my shoulders. While part of me is terrified, the other part of me knows I'm doing this for the right reasons.

In the end this will either work or it won't, and I plan to give it my all.

"WHAT ABOUT THIS?" Ruby asks, holding up a shirt I haven't worn in two years.

"Donate, I haven't been that skinny in a long time. Not since I quit coaching softball."

Mom makes a noise. "Why *did* you quit coaching softball?"

"There was this guy coaching one of the other teams. He gave me the creeps, and he would somehow always be at the same ballfield I was at. One day he didn't show up, I got curious and looked on the internet. He was arrested for assaulting a woman in the bathroom at one of the county parks." I shiver as I tell them the story. "After that, it kind of lost some of its appeal."

"I can see why." Ruby makes a face. "Why are there such weirdos in this world? It makes me nervous with Molly. Like Caleb is already talking about when she starts dating, he's going to follow the car."

I laugh loudly. "He has plenty of practice. He did that to me, when I went on my first couple of dates."

Mom laughs along with me. "You never told me that."

I shrug, a warmth flowing through me as I think about my

older brother. "It made me feel good to know he was there if I needed him. He never got out of line, never made his presence known, and didn't cause an issue. I appreciated it."

"He's such a good brother," Mom grins.

"He is, sometimes he's annoying, but for the most part, I wouldn't trade him for anything."

We're going through the last of my closet when my phone buzzes in my pocket. Taking it out, I see Nick's sent me a text.

N: Get here soon, please. My mom just showed up with a fucking list. And make no mistake about it. Whitney Kepler expects to get this shit done tonight. This list is bigger than my grocery list.

K: LOL! What am I supposed to do? She'll probably put me to work as soon as I walk through the door.

N: No she won't, I've already explained you're moving your stuff in, and when you get here I need to help you. Get here so I can help you!

K: I'll be about forty-five more minutes. We have just a few more things to go through.

N: Hurry, please!

This will probably be the only time in my life that Nick asks me to hurry for anything, but the truth is I'll take it. Looking into what was my bedroom, I see we're done with the closet and the small dresser I had. Now it's time for the bathroom. Once this is done, it'll be time to leave, time to move on to the next step in my life.

"We'll take these downstairs to your car while you pack up the bathroom," Ruby tells me as she hauls a box up.

"Great idea, I won't be long."

Fifteen minutes later they've taken the boxes downstairs and my bathroom doesn't look like mine any longer. I walk through the place one more time, touching things here and there, memories crawling through my mind. This was the first apartment that was ever mine. I moved from my parent's house right into here with Stella.

I was so proud for it to be ours; we decorated, budgeted to afford everything that would turn it from an apartment into a home, and sometimes ate ramen because we were both broke. Stella fell in love and married while she was here. I fell in love, and now I'm moving in with the man who holds my heart. While I'm sad to be leaving this place that's meant so much to me over the past few years, I'm excited to be moving on.

As weird as it sounds, I've been hanging onto this apartment like a kite being pulled from my hands by a strong wind. It was the only thing that was mine. Now it'll be Cutter's.

Walking to the door for the last time, I take a look around before I turn off the light and close the door. Cutter's coming over after he gets off his midnight shift, and this will be his.

"Bye," I whisper, tears in my eyes.

It's almost like I'm saying goodbye to a little piece of myself, and as I close the door, I know without a doubt I'll never be able to get that Kelsea back. This one is ready to fight for everything that's hers, damn anyone who stands in the way.

SIXTEEN

Whitney

I'm nervous as I stand outside the door of my son's apartment. Anyone probably would be, especially if they were about to bulldoze their way into his life. My stomach churns as I knock on the door, not because I'm scared of him, but because I know he's so private. He likes to live his life on his terms, has been like that since we adopted him.

The door opens, and a slight grin kicks up the side of his mouth. The smile I've only seen him smile at me. Sometimes I get the feeling he tolerates certain people, but I truly believe this kid loves his family. "Momma?"

"Hey." I give him a smile back. "I hope you aren't busy."

His eyes are wide, and I can tell he wants to be busy, but knowing him, his apartment is immaculate.

"Can I come in?" He can never tell me no, and I'm fully aware of it.

"Sure." He holds the door open for me.

I go in, immediately sitting on the couch. "Your dad told me what's going on with this boy. I have to tell you, Nick, what you're doing is amazing." I reach into my purse. "But I wonder if you know exactly what you've gotten yourself into."

"Let me guess, you have a list of things you think I may not know?"

Smirking at him, I put the paper down on the coffee table. "Busted, and I know you're going to tell me you're an adult."

"I am."

"And you don't need my help."

"That's where you're wrong Mom, I'm gonna need everyone's help. I do know what I'm getting myself into because I've been Darren before. What I don't know is the logistics. Like how am I going to provide him with all the things you and Dad provided to me?"

Reaching over, I grab his hand, squeezing strongly, hoping to give him some of the strength he so desperately needs. "You have it all inside you, Nick. You're a good man."

His voice is ragged when he speaks. "No, I'm a fucked-up kid who grew into a man that still has nightmares sometimes. When the walls close in, I still sleep on the goddamned balcony. I mean, what do I think I'm doing here?"

My heart breaks for him. Ever since the day he came to live with us, all I've wanted to do is make life easier on him. Make it to where he didn't have to wonder day-to-day where his next meal or new clothes were coming from. Looking back, I wonder if I failed to make him feel safe.

"The walls close in on all of us from time to time, Nick. Sometimes we all feel suffocated. When your dad does, he goes to his shop. When I do, I make plans, because that's what I've always done. You don't have to have all the answers. None of us do – we just get by with what we can, but I promise you, you're the best person to take care of this boy, because you've been there."

He lifts his eyes up to mine, and I see the lost, vulnerable little boy he was back then. "And you have help from what I hear. Kelsea will be here with you, too."

"Yeah," he answers, but doesn't look completely happy about it.

"What's going on with you and Kelsea?"

"That shit got complicated as fuck too. I've known for years she's liked me, I've liked her too, but I could never understand why she'd want to slum with me."

My hand grasping his tightly squeezes in reflex to what he's just said. "Slumming with you? Stop it now. You're worthy, Nickolas."

"Not of that girl." His voice has a tell-all grin in it. "She would move mountains to be with me, when all I've given her is a small piece of myself."

"That girl is the girl you need," I argue. "She's going to fight not only for you, but *with* you, in whatever you want."

"She's moving in tonight," he admits. "Didn't even think about it twice."

"She's strong," I remind him. "Look who her family is. Nothing was easy for Mason, not even when he met Karina. They've made a good life together, and they've raised a daughter who knows her own mind. Kelsea might be willing to do a lot for you, Nick, but she's not willing to risk herself for you. It's important you remember that. If she's coming here to help you, then she's here to help you."

"I know, I'm just not used to the help, ya know?"

I laugh, shaking my head. "If anyone knows, it's me. I remember putting brand new clothes in your room the first night you were there, and you refused to wear them for months, because you didn't want to ruin them."

He laughs along with me. "I'd never had name brand. I was

scared to death I'd get something on them and then get my ass beat because I'd ruined them."

Putting my hand behind his neck, I force my son to look at me. "But we got over that. You learned you'd get yelled at for a missed curfew, or a class you didn't take seriously, not because you stained a shirt. You'll learn this. All these things Darren will need, you have inside you, and for the hard parts you have Kelsea here to back you up. If there's one thing I've always wanted you to know, it's that your beginnings didn't define you. Nick Cooper might be who you started out as, but you ended up Nick Kepler, and with that you gained more than you ever lost."

I'm crying now, and his eyes are misty. Maybe we've needed to say these words to each other for a long time, maybe I've just been assuming he knows how much he's loved.

"One of the greatest joys of my life has been being your mother. After Stella, we tried to have another, but it just didn't work out. The moment I heard about you, I knew it was because you were meant to be in our lives. I am just as proud of you as I am of Stella."

"I know." He grabs my hand in his, sniffling slightly. "The one thing you gave me that I've been thankful for as I grew up is that you never treated me differently than her. If she got in trouble for something, so did I when I did it. If she got praised for doing something, then if I did it, I got praised, too. You taught me how to be fair."

"What do you mean to be fair?" I have a sinking suspicion I know what he means, but I need for him to clarify it.

"With my birth mom, it was all about getting back at me. If I caused what she perceived to be a problem, she'd make a problem for me, even bigger than the one I supposedly caused. That's what I learned. There was never fairness nor forgiveness, and there sure as fuck wasn't any sportsmanship taught to me before I came to live with you. Not only did your family save my life, but they taught me how to be a good person. I have no doubt I'd end up in the back of a police car instead of driving one if it hadn't been for you. All of that? That's what I want to do for Darren, and I thank you for giving me the foundation to be able to."

I'm crying now, ugly tears sliding down my face as I reach forward, gathering him in my arms. "You were the best gift we ever got, that we didn't know we needed," I whisper to him, because I want him to know it. We were okay being a one-child family, we'd adjusted to it and could have lived our entire lives like that, but as soon as we learned about Nick, it was like we were called to a higher power.

Pulling away, I wipe my face.

"So what's all this?" He picks up my list.

"Numbers you may need, things you may have forgotten about, things I found helpful. I didn't want you to have to search all of that out on your own. I put it all together. Obviously you don't have to use it, if you don't want to, but I thought it'd be helpful."

He looks down, flipping through the pages. "There's a lot here I didn't think about, believe it or not. I really appreciate this."

"Whatever you need, please let me know."

"He'll need clothes." He winks at me.

I laugh loudly. "Clothes are damn expensive for kids."

"Exactly, and since you're a surrogate grandma right now, isn't it your place to spoil the kid?"

"Look at you, already learning. You'll be great at this, Nick, and whatever you don't get, Kelsea will. The two of you are going to make a great team."

"Speaking of." He picks his phone up as it buzzes. "She's on her way."

"Alright, I'll get out of your hair. I love you."

He stands up, walking me to the door. When we get there, he opens his arms up wide, hugging me tightly. "Love you too, Momma. Thanks for taking a chance on me."

Pulling back, I kiss him on the cheek. "Best chance I ever took."

SEVENTEEN

Kelsea

The last two days have been the longest of my life as Nick and I have prepared to go before the judge. From what we heard, his dad was served and he'll be appearing. I'm not sure how I feel about that exactly. He's always been a faceless enemy to me.

Nick and I sit in the court room; we're not allowed to sit next to our attorney, but we're in the front row, right behind him. Nick looks spectacular in his uniform, and I took extra care with my dress and curling my hair this morning.

Yesterday we had the home visit, which expedited us to serve as foster parents to Darren, and I'm scared to death we won't leave here with him today.

"You okay?" Nick asks as he leans in.

"Scared to death they'll think we aren't the best thing for him," I admit, my hand shaking slightly as I smooth my dress over my thighs.

He reaches over, grabbing my hand in his. The warmth feels fills a spot in my body that's been cold for longer than I can remember. "We've got this." He smiles widely at me, one dimple popping on his left cheek.

"Are you faking it 'til you make it?" I whisper. "You can tell me, I won't blow your cover."

"Like a motherfucker. I'm scared to death."

And that admission right there is why I love Nick. "Same," I agree.

He takes his hand from mine, putting his arm around my neck before leaning in, dropping a kiss on my forehead. These tender moments while unexpected, also give me hope. Hope we can move past where we are and maybe, just maybe, be the family we're pretending to be.

The court is asked to be vacated as they explain there is a minor involved. We keep our seats, but I feel Nick stiffen. When I follow where he's looking at, I see a man who looks like life has beaten him down, dressed in jeans and an old University of Tennessee t-shirt. There are stains on both the jeans and the t-shirt, his hair is disheveled, and it smells as if he hasn't had a shower in a few days. He's definitely been on a bender. I grab Nick's arm as the man looks over at us, smiling.

That smile though, it's not the type I'm used to getting from older men. This one gives me the creeps, I shiver at the thought of being alone with him. "Is that his dad?" I ask quietly.

"Yup, that's the son of a bitch," Nick answers just as quietly.

I force an impassive look on my face; I don't want him to know he gets to me. Even when I hear the judge ask if he has an attorney. Learning that his name is Ezra bothers me since that's biblical and this man standing in front of us? He's way more sinner than saint.

"No sir, I don't have counsel," he answers, looking back at us.

I listen intensely as they call our counsel, explaining that

Nick and I want to take custody of Darren. With pride I hear them talk about Nick being a decorated officer and the certifications I've been able to accomplish while working. I'm proud of us, how far we've come. Even though we both had great parents, that's not an automatic road to winning at life. We've still had to work very hard.

"They agree to take custody of this child?" the judge asks our attorney.

"Yes, your honor." He shuffles some papers in front of him. "They've both had the required courses from the state because of their professions, the home visit was done yesterday. They are certified."

"Mr. Metcalfe, I'm looking at your history here. You've been arrested numerous times, and accused even more times of harming your son. What do you have to say for that?"

"He's got a smart mouth. I grew up the way he has, and I don't see anything wrong with me."

I gasp because no matter how smart someone's mouth is, they don't deserve what this child has lived through. Beside me Nick is tightly wound, I legitimately think the only reason he's still sitting here is because I'm resting my hand on his thigh.

"What a fucker," he growls.

"That's the problem, Mr. Metcalfe. Obviously you and I have very different expectations on how to care for a child. Because the court believes it's typically in the best interest of the child to have their biological parents, I'm going to ask you two things. Number one, where is the mother?"

He cocks his head to the side. "Dead. Drug overdose when he was three. He don't even remember her."

I tip my head back trying to hold back the tears. This kills me to hear these words come so matter-of-factly from this man. The judge makes some notes in his notebook.

"I'm going to give you ninety days, Mr. Metcalfe. The child

will remain with the foster parents, while you prove to me you can be his father. You'll have certain goals to meet. There will be home visits, anger management, and I'm expecting you to do all of this, show me you want to keep your child. If you're in trouble before the ninety days are up? This child will go to Mr. Kepler and Ms. Harrison permanently. If in the allotted time you haven't completed what I've asked? The child will go to Mr. Kepler and Ms. Harrison permanently. Do you understand?"

He doesn't speak, just nods his head as he looks at me and Nick. I still don't like the way he's looking at me, and I can tell Nick doesn't either.

"If I may say something?" he asks the court. "Why is he being placed in a home where they aren't married? Doesn't that set an even worse example than I was?"

"Seeing as how there was a home visit, no drugs were found and neither of them have a documented history of beating a child, I think the fact they aren't yet married isn't as much of a problem for the court as you are. They're in a committed relationship, and for now that pleases the court." He bangs his gavel. "Ninety days, Mr. Metcalfe. I'll be watching."

As the judge leaves, he walks by Nick and I.

"He may be watching me, but you can bet your ass, I'll be watching y'all."

Nick gets up, walking over to where he stands. I follow because I don't know what else to do. "Make a threat against me, I'm begging you to."

"Have no doubt I'll be gunning for you, motherfucker. He's my ticket. You don't get it, do you?"

"I don't," I pipe up. I don't understand if he obviously doesn't care for Darren, why is Darren so important? "So why don't you explain it to me."

He looks at Nick and then back at me. "Oh I get it. You got yourself a rich bitch," he laughs.

Nick makes a noise, but I put my hand on his shoulder, trying to prevent him from making this worse than it already is.

"She didn't grow up in the system like us, did she?"

He looks me up and down, which makes me cross my arms around my midsection. "Because Darren is such a slow fuckin' kid and he doesn't have mommy dearest around anymore, I was getting almost two grand a month for his sorry ass. The two of you? You've fucked that up for me, but don't think I won't fix this."

"If you worked as hard at keeping a job as you do cheating the goddamn system, you'd be a hell of a person." Nick levels him with a glare. "This child, he isn't a meal ticket for you. He's your flesh and blood. He came from you, how can you say he's your meal ticket?"

"Same way your mama did." He grins.

I can almost feel the anger radiating off of Nick's body. "C'mon, let's get out of here." I push him toward the exit, hoping we don't make a scene.

"Remember where you came from, Nick *Cooper*."

We hear him until the door shuts. Outside, Darren's attorney is waiting with our attorney. "Alright, let's go get him."

As we follow these two people who've made it their job to make sure justice is served, I feel like I'm about to puke. My life has never been what I would call exciting, but I have a feeling all of that? It's about to change right now.

EIGHTEEN

Nick

To say I'm nervous would be an understatement. Darren rides in the back seat of my extended cab truck. I wasn't precisely sure if we'd leave court with him today, but after meeting with the foster family who was taking care of him at the attorney's office, here we are.

I'd be lying if I said we were completely comfortable with one another right now. To be honest, this ride is downright painful. Luckily for me, Kels can talk to a fucking brick wall.

"Are you excited to start a new school? You'll have quasi-relations there. My niece and nephew go to the one you're going to go to, and my mom teaches for the district. She used to teach high school, but last year she took a position that allows her to go into all classes and observe. So you may see her, too. Eventually you'll meet everybody, but I can assure you my niece and nephew are the cream of the crop." She grins proudly back at him. I can see that even from where I sit.

"That's good." Darren speaks softly. "I didn't have too

many friends at my old school. People didn't like my dad, and I never had cool clothes."

"You're in luck, both of our parents," – she points between me and her – "are super excited to welcome you into our families. We're going to have dinner with them tonight at Nick's parents' house. I've heard there's some gifts for you there."

"Gifts?" I can hear the excitement in his voice.

It fucking guts me because I know exactly what he's gone through. So many birthdays and holidays, he probably saw all the kids at school come the next day in all their new shit. Yet, there he was, trying to make a small pair of shoes last another month, trying to make sure his one good shirt stayed pristine.

"So many gifts you'll think it's Christmas." I smile at him in the rearview. "You have a ton of people who are very excited to meet you."

"Why?"

At first I had asked the same thing, why would someone be interested in me after my parents hadn't been interested in me. I struggled with the same questions.

"Because they love us, and we care for you. It's what family does," Kelsea answers.

"Is that true?" he asks me.

"It is, and you'll see how true it is the longer you're around us. We have a large, obnoxious family. They sometimes get on our nerves, but they love us."

"What's that like?" Darren asks quietly.

I hear Kelsea make a noise in her throat. Reaching over I grab her hand in mine. She's never dealt with someone like this, I know it's hard to even believe people live like this. It's up to me to answer this question.

"It's the best feeling in the world."

"HE SEEMS to be handling it well." Ransom nods over to where Darren is sitting with my dad and Kelsea's nephew, playing some video game.

"He does," I agree. "I thought for a minute when he saw the amount of gifts he was gonna cry or hyperventilate."

"Hell, I thought I was going to, too," Ransom laughs. "It's amazing how lucky we are. The family we have is one of the best."

"Here, here." I lift my can of Coke up to his. "How's Stelle?"

"Working on her second plate of cake, so I'm assuming she's doing awesome." He laughs.

"Don't mention that second plate of cake."

"Fuck no," he shakes his head. "I've learned very quickly what I'm supposed to say and what I'm not supposed to say."

We're laughing when I hear a throat clear behind me.

"Ransom, you mind if I have a conversation with Nick?"

There's no one I respect more than my dad, no one except Mason "Menace" Harrison. I've been waiting on this, and I knew it was coming soon. Kelsea is his baby girl, and I've known he's wanted to say his peace.

"Mason." I nod to him.

He nods back, and I wait patiently, hoping like hell he doesn't notice my hand shaking as it holds my can. "I've been waiting on you." I take a drink.

"Bet you have. Honestly, I only have two things to say to you, and you're free to say to me what you want. Two things, Nick. That woman will always be my little girl. You treat her with respect and you don't lie to her. I'm not getting in the middle of your relationship because she knows her own mind, and if I ever tried to butt in, she'd hand me my ass on a platter."

"She would," I agree.

"Promise me." He holds out his hand.

"I promise to respect her, not to lie to her, and protect her. She could have done so many other things when I asked her for help. She's basically put her life on hold to help me give him a good life. I'll never forget it. I've never had a friend like her."

Mason looks over at her, smiling while she rubs Stella's non-existent baby belly. "She loves you, and if you aren't able to return that feeling, believe it or not, I do understand, but don't ever pretend to be something you're not for her."

I'm sweating because he can see me so clearly. Things I've tried to hide from others. He's so much like the daughter we're talking about. "You have my word. You know there are lots of situations in my life where my word wouldn't count for shit, but I promise you, she'll be taken care of."

"That's all I need to hear from you." He puts his hand on my shoulder. "Your word is good enough for me, but just know, you fuck up? I'll be right there, ready to make you wish you hadn't."

"Completely understood, Mason. I don't want to hurt her."

"Then we're on the same page, and I thank you. What the two of you have decided to do is wonderful, and I think we all have a little bit of a stake in it." He moves his hand around the room, indicating everyone whose come out for this dinner/welcoming party for Darren.

He leaves me, going over to talk with Havoc and Leigh. Looking around, I realize everyone in this room is considered a friend of ours and how lucky we are. There were moments in my life where I have been able to count my friends on one hand, and it was too many fingers. All the people here, tonight? They're my family and I wouldn't trade it for the world.

The best part about this? I get to introduce Darren into the best family anyone could ever ask for.

NINETEEN

Kelsea

"Is he asleep?" I ask Nick later on that night.

The two of us are getting ready for bed, and I have to smile at the picture of domesticity we make. Who would have thought a month ago, I'd be sitting on his bed putting moisturizer on my face while he came out of the shower, a towel wrapped around his waist, a kid asleep in the bedroom a little down the hallway from ours.

"Out like a light. He didn't even move when I went in to turn his light off." Nick uses another towel to dry off his hair.

I take that moment to look at him. His skin holds a slight tan all year round, and it's obvious he's worked hard on his body. It's cut in places I didn't even know it could be cut, the vee leading down behind the towel is enticing enough it makes me want to follow the path with my tongue.

He's got his signature scruffy – not quite a beard, but not clean-shaven face. His biceps and forearms ripple as he vigorously works the towel through his dark locks.

When he stops, he drops both towels where he stands. I inhale sharply.

"Don't worry, Kels, I'll clean up my mess in the morning." He yawns loudly. "Too tired to do it right now."

"Trust me, I didn't make that noise because of you throwing your towel on the floor."

He turns, a grin on his face, his eyes showing interest. "What did you make it for then?"

I roll my eyes. "Give me a break, you know you're hot as hell."

He flexes his hands, causing his forearms to tighten, and I do my best not to fall in a puddle at his feet. "If I wasn't so tired tonight, Kels, I'd completely take advantage of how much you seem to love my body."

"If I wasn't so tired, I'd let you," I fire back at him.

We watch each other as we pull down the covers, getting ready for bed. He's fallen asleep with me every night since I moved in, and I've only caught him not here in the morning twice. This time, I lie down, pulling the covers over me while he turns out the lights.

There's a dip in the mattress as he gets in. I can feel him turn over, and when the heat of his breath hits my neck, I know he's facing me. His arms go around me; for a moment I stiffen because we haven't done this before.

"Do you mind? I want to be close to you tonight."

"Nick." I lean in, kissing him softly on the lips. "You never have to ask. Your arms are the safest place I've ever been and my favorite place to be."

He inhales deeply. "You could kill me, Kels. You know that, right? You make me want to give you everything, let all my guards down, and just lay myself bare to you."

"You could kill me too, so I guess we're even."

For a long time neither of us speaks, and as we drift off, I hold on tightly to the man holding me in his arms.

TIRED DOESN'T EVEN BEGIN to cover how I feel. Who knew being the guardian of a pre-teen kid was so exhausting? I'm on my second cup of coffee this morning. Nick's already left for the day, and I'm struggling to pack Darren's lunch. He comes in wearing some of the new clothes he got at his welcome dinner.

"Looking slick." I whistle. "Those shoes are awesome." I look down at a pair of basketball shoes on his feet.

"I think so." He blushes. "I've never had shoes this nice before."

"Dude, I don't think I've had shoes that nice before." I laugh a little crazy-like because I'm so tired. "But my brother is going to love spoiling you. I do it to his kids all the time. Are you and Molly getting along?" They're in the same grade, but I'm not positive if they're in the same class or not.

"Molly's great." He pulls a bowl out of the dishwasher, sits it on the table, and then goes to get the cereal we've learned he loves. "She lets me hang out with her at lunch and in the morning before classes start."

"That's awesome, remember you're going home with her today since me and Nick will both be at work a little later today. Are you cool with going to Caleb's?"

"Yeah, he played video games with me the other day, told me we'd be able to have a rematch." He pours milk over his cereal, sits down, and begins to eat. "I'm looking forward to it."

"Just make sure you do your homework first. That's a rule in their house, just like it's a rule here."

I'm inhaling coffee, hoping it will wake me up, so that I'm

not walking around like a zombie today. Zoning out, I'm mentally going over my day, trying to imagine what I have before me.

"Kelsea, can I ask you a question?"

"Sure." I set my coffee cup down before I pull out the chair next to him and have a seat.

"What was it like growing up with a brother? I always wondered what it would be like having a brother or sister?"

He's so inquisitive about mostly everything, and he's not scared to ask questions. In fact, we encourage it, so I'm thankful he feels comfortable enough to do it.

"It's kind of different in my situation," I explain. "Caleb had already moved out when I was born. While he was there whenever I needed him to be, he didn't live in the house with us. I do have to admit it was fun going to his apartment and then his house after he married Ruby. They didn't have the same rules my mom and dad did."

"Like you got to stay up past your bedtime and eat what you wanted?"

I laugh at how innocent he can be. "Yeah, exactly that. We'd stay up late watching movies, and he'd let me pick my dinner. It was fun, because those were things my parents wouldn't let me do."

He looks down at his cereal, twirling his spoon in the milk. "Do you think I'll ever be a big brother?" he asks quietly.

The truth is I don't know how to answer this question. Things are so up in the air between Nick and I, we aren't sure how long we'll get to keep Darren, and who knows what's going to happen in the future. I feel bad because there's no good answer.

"I would say none of us know what the future will bring."

"So you and Nick aren't gonna get married?" His eyebrows are drawn together in confusion.

Man, I wish he were here to help me out with this. "Nick and I are working through our relationship, but no matter what happens, you will always be our number one priority.

He seems to mull that over in his head before he takes another bite of cereal and opens the iPad Caleb gave him to play with. Letting out a breath, I pat

myself on the back for handling this completely by myself. Quickly I make waffles, eat them, and then get Darren herded to the front door.

"Got all your stuff for school today?"

"Yup." He shows me his backpack. "Did all my homework and Nick signed my weekly planner," he confirms.

"Alright, let's get you to school and me to work."

When we pull out of the parking lot right on time, I know today is gonna be a good day.

TWENTY

Nick

When I hear the address come over the scanner, I know I shouldn't respond, but I'm the closest one to the scene. Something churns in my gut telling me not to respond. It's been two weeks since Darren moved in with us. We're finally getting into a routine, and I think he's learning what it's like to have people who care about him. He's more trusting than I ever was, and I hope it lasts. I know I'm learning what it is to care for other people too. But this? I really shouldn't do it.

"Is there anyone closer than me, dispatch?"

"Negative Nick, you're the closest. There's been another call about him disturbing the peace."

Fuck me running.

"Show me as responding."

"I'll be about five minutes behind." I hear Ransom.

That gives me a little bit of comfort, but I know this isn't going to go smoothly. Pulling into the neighborhood, I feel the cloud of despair fall over me, a darkness that I just never can seem to get away from. That darkness is why I sleep outside sometimes.

"Dispatch, I'm making contact."

Stopping in front of the house, I can see Ezra. He's standing outside ranting and raving at his neighbors. They're screaming from their spot across the yard. Something tells me this won't be easy. When I get out, I tighten my form and do my best to appear like I'm not bothered to be here.

"They sent you?" He takes a drink of the beer can in his hand. "Of all people, they sent you?"

"We don't get to pick and choose our calls. We just kinda of get to make sure the public is safe and taken care of."

"Safe and taken care of?" He throws his beer can down.

Instead of reprimanding him about littering, I watch as he puts his hand in his pocket.

"Get your hands out of your pockets."

"Just getting me some chew." He holds up a can of Skoal.

He puts a pouch in between his lip and teeth.

"Why are people calling you in?" I ask, resting my palm on the butt of my gun.

"Just having a disagreement."

"Ma'am, can you come over here?" I point to his neighbor.

My eyes watch her as she comes over. She looks like one of the good ones. She's wearing a uniform for one of the local factories and she looks tired as hell. Like life has beaten her the fuck down and she's not sure she'll ever be able to come back from it. She stands beside me, I can see the fear in her body language, so I put myself in between the two of them.

"Can you tell me what's going on here?"

"He's drunk, again." She points to Ezra. "When he gets drunk, he comes out here and starts yelling, then he starts throwing shit. Now that he doesn't have his son to terrorize, he's going to do it to the whole damn neighborhood."

"Shut your fuckin' mouth or I'll shut it for you." He lunges at her, but I grab him by his shirt, hauling him back.

"You need to calm down." I push him farther away.

In my peripheral vision, I see Ransom pull up. Thank God. "Want me to separate them?"

"He's drunk," she yells.

"She's a bitch," he yells back.

Ransom pushes Ezra to the side, I take the woman, pulling her a little farther away. "What can we do to help you?"

She crosses her arms, looking pissed. "He does this every night. Last night, he chucked a brick through my son's bedroom window. He's lucky my son wasn't in bed."

"Did you call the police last night?"

She breathes heavily. "No, typically I don't want to ever get involved. It's easier in this neighborhood not to get involved. Tonight he kept looking at every kid who rode by on their bike and he was screaming shit. It scared me. His poor son took all his anger, and now he's not there anymore, I'm worried he'll do something to one of the other kids." She runs a hand through hair that's about three months overdue for a color. "I couldn't do anything to help his son, but I'll be damned if I sit around and watch him scare every kid in this neighborhood."

Scribbling in my notebook, I do my best to keep my own feelings out of this. I can feel her eyes on me, and I'm wondering what she's seeing.

"He's told everybody about you, ya know? Not personally but you've been his biggest source of complaint as he screams. He enjoys telling people a cop from this neighborhood has his son. He says he's going to kill you."

"He can try." I don't know whether I'm telling myself that, or telling her.

"If you don't calm down, you're taking a ride," Ransom speaks loudly to Ezra.

"Fuck you!" It's then I see him spit on Ransom's shoes.

Within the blink of an eye, Ransom's got him on the ground, a knee in his back, pulling his hands behind him, cuffing tightly. When Ransom pulls him up, Ezra looks at me. "I'll kill you, you took my family away from me. I'll fucking end you. Don't think I can't."

He's still screaming as Ransom puts him in the back of another patrol car that's come to assist us. As he pulls away, I can't get those words out of my head.

TWO HOURS LATER, I'm entering my apartment. Things have changed in such a short amount of time. It used to be I'd come home to silence, no matter the hour. Tonight it's six p.m., and there's noise, including laughter, coming from the kitchen.

I do my routine of placing my gun in a lockbox before I announce myself. "What's going on in here to cause all this laughing?"

"We're making a cake." Darren giggles as he sticks his finger in the batter.

"He said he'd never done it before, and I mean, everyone should make a cake and scoop up some of the batter. Wanna help?" She winks, sticking her finger in the batter, before she brings it up to her mouth, making a show of licking it off her finger.

Kels and I, we haven't had a lot of time alone since Darren came to live with us. My dick jumps against my zipper and I'm possibly harder than I've ever been. I walk over, standing behind her as I wrap my arms around her waist, leaning forward to take hold of her finger in my mouth.

I know the second she feels my arousal against her ass. She melts against me, swirling my tongue around, I gather the batter, sucking strongly before letting it go. "That's good, can't wait until it's cooked."

Darren is oblivious to the sexual attraction stretched between the two of us. Which is probably good for him. I let her go, watching as the two of them transfer the batter to two round cake pans. She looks at Darren.

"You have about twenty-five minutes before these get done, time for you to take a shower, dude."

She puts them in the oven, and then gives him a pointed look. When he runs off, she grabs my hand, pulling me down the hallway. She waits until the bathroom door slams shut, before grinning and pulling me into our bedroom. The door shuts with a soft click as she turns around, pushes me against it, and hits her knees right in front of me.

Reaching over, she gives the lock a turn, and then goes to work on my belt.

"Kels, what the fuck?" I'm asking as she gets my belt off, zipper down, and button undone.

"If you have to ask, I'm doing it wrong." She grins before sticking her hand into my tented briefs, dragging my cock out.

The head is sensitive as it brushes against the cotton, causing me to groan. "Oh shit," I groan when she licks the underside up to the tip, taking it in her mouth. My fingers dig into her hair, holding her right where I need her to be. "Is this okay?" I ask as my hips start a rhythm that I can't seem to stop.

She pulls back, leaving my length in the cool air of the bedroom. "I want this, Nick. When I felt this against me, all I wanted to do was give you pleasure. I'm so wet right now." She closes her eyes, licking my tip again. "But I know we don't have time."

"The fuck we don't." I lift her up by her hair. She shivers as I make quick work of her sweatpants and the little scrap of lace she calls underwear.

Laying down on the bed, I motion to her. "C'mere, Kels."

"What do you want?"

I love that she's still a little innocent when it comes to certain things. It makes teaching her so fucking fun. "Sit on my face and suck my cock at the same time."

Her eyes grow wide when she realizes what I'm telling her to do.

"We don't have much time." She pulls her lip between her teeth.

"Trust me." I palm my length. "This won't take long."

With my big hands, I help her straddle my face as she leans down to take my length down her throat. She goes to work on me, and I go to work on her, sucking on her clit, rubbing my tongue against her wet folds. She's moaning against my dick, causing it to jump every time I feel it rubbing the back of her throat. She wasn't lying when she said she was wet. My girl is soaking the fuck out of my face, out of the finger I'm pressing into her softness, taking it with a hunger she probably didn't even know she had.

I can feel her thighs, tightening against me. "Feel good?" I ask as I pull my face back slightly.

"Yes," she moans when I go back to work. Lick, suck, finger. Lick, suck, finger. She's rocking against my tongue, taking me deeper and deeper, speeding up as I do the same. I can feel her body stiffen, can tell she's almost there.

"Come on, Kels," I encourage her, rubbing my thumb against her clit, feeling the suction growing stronger on my cock. "C'mon baby, is this it?" I quicken my pace. "Right there?" And if my dick wasn't in her mouth she'd alert the whole apartment building to what we're doing. "Yeah, babe, ride it out." She's undulating against me.

I pick up my pace against her, fucking her face with the taste of her on my tongue and the scent of her in my nose.

"Oh fuck," I groan, arching my back up off the bed as I spill against her tongue.

We're both gasping like we just ran a marathon, but damned if I'm ever going to be able to wipe the goofy smile off my face.

TWENTY-ONE

Nick

"Hey, I'm leaving for work," I hear the whispered voice of Kelsea.

"Yeah?" I answer, trying desperately to wake myself up. "What time is it?"

"Five-thirty," she answers, as she goes to the closet, bends down, and comes back over to the bed. She has a seat, as she goes about putting her shoes on. "Remember, I have an early shift today because we're doing the free clinic? You have to get Darren to school for me."

Typically she gets him off to school and I pick him up. We've settled into a nice routine, and so far things have been working well. The problem with today is, I just got off-shift at three. "What time do I have to wake him up?" I yawn as I push myself up onto my hand.

"Six-twenty," she answers, reaching in to muss my hair. "You have to leave here by seven to get him there on time, so don't let him jerk you around."

"Will he do that?"

"With his breakfast, yes. He'll keep telling you it's okay for him to have Pop Tarts. That's not the case, he can't have that much sugar, or he will bounce off the walls and be very difficult to go into the school."

I'm doing my best to follow along but morning isn't my normal routine and fuck if I'm not tired. "So what can he eat?"

"I laid out a banana and put the cereal in a container for you. Just open the container, put milk in it, and cut up his banana. He can have a cup of juice if he wants."

"Okay," I rub my face. "I might as well try to wake up."

"I'm really sorry today worked out like this. I know you're tired." She cups my cheek with the palm of her hand.

"Not your fault," I can't help but turn into her caress. "Wish I could get you to tuck back in here with me."

She giggles and grins. "Stop trying to sweet talk me."

"Is it working?"

She leans in, kissing me softly. "Probably better than you think, but I gotta go."

"Be safe today."

"You too," she blows me a kiss as she leaves.

Groaning, I get up and get going so I can help him prepare for the day.

"I DON'T WANT THIS CEREAL," Darren pouts as he crosses his arms in front of him. "Kels always gives me Pop Tarts."

Sighing, I do my best not to lose my temper. I'm tired, hungry, and not in the mood to deal with his attitude. "She told me you get the cereal. So you're going to eat the cereal."

He frowns, and I do my best not to show my irritation. This

is the first time he's gotten attitude with me, but I'm aware he's thrown it at Kels a few times. It's not unusual. He's had a lot of changes the past few months, and not every day can be good.

"I don't want it," he sets his jaw looking at me.

"You're going to eat it."

"No I'm not," he picks it up, throwing it across the room.

Luckily I hadn't put milk in it yet. The two of us face off with one another. His chest is pumping up and down as he looks at me. Calmly I reach into the cabinet, pulling out the box of cereal. "You're going to clean that up."

"What are you going to do to me if I don't?"

"You'll be grounded from playing video games tonight."

"How will Kelsea know?" He raises and eyebrow at me.

"Kelsea and I are a team, and you know we are. As soon as I drop you off, I'll call her, explain about this temper tantrum and tell her you're grounded. Because we're a team, she'll back me up. You'll go straight to your room after dinner."

"Why?" He hitches his chin in defiance. "So you can beat me without her seeing?"

Sighing I tilt my head back. He's so much like me. "Look, I know what you're trying to do. You're trying to push me to my limit. Trying to see what's going to happen when I get angry, because you want to see if I'm like your dad. I'm not, and you'll never push me that far. I can promise you that."

"How do you know?" He asks softly. "Sometimes I get so angry I want to hit something."

"I do too," the honesty ripping me apart. "But I know what happens when you hit another person. Instead I do things with my hands, I go out on the balcony and take a breather. If I'm really pissed I go play basketball, beat the fuck out that ball until I'm done," I walk over to where he is, bending down so we can look in each other's eyes. "You can be angry without hitting or hurting another person. I promise."

Without warning, he begins sobbing, throwing himself into my arms. "I'm sorry," he wails.

"It's okay, you had to test me. I get it."

He pulls back, nodding with a sob. "Am I still in trouble?"

"Yeah, you are. We don't have time to clean it up this morning, so you'll clean it up when you come home tonight. Go wash your face and I'll fix you a bowl to go and you can eat on the way to school."

He nods, but before he leaves the room, I hear his soft voice. "Nick?"

"Yeah, buddy?"

"Thank you," the smile he gives me is the best one I've seen from him.

"No problem. You've always got me. No matter what."

When he walks towards the bathroom, he does so with his shoulders squared and his head held high. Not gonna lie, it's the best thing I've seen since he moved in with us.

Kelsea

It's a cloudy afternoon in Laurel Springs. Checking my phone, I make sure I haven't missed a text from Caleb. We're meeting for lunch, but he's ten minutes late.

Sighing when I don't see a text, I crane my neck to look out the window. Leighton puts a glass of iced tea in front of me. "Thank you, I'm so thirsty today."

"It never fails, when you're being stood up for lunch, you're always more thirsty," she winks at me. "I saw Caleb pull up as I walked over here."

I giggle. "Thanks, I did think he was about to stand me up."

The bell over the door rings, announcing someone entering. Sure enough, it's my older brother. He plants a kiss on Leigh's cheek before he slides in the booth across from me.

"Large water and some m'fing cheese fries," he grins over at me.

"Caleb," I whine. "You know I'm trying to eat better."

"And you know," he whines back. "That the only time I get to eat like this is when I come out with you. Cheer up buttercup, and eat the calories with me."

I roll my eyes to the side. "Bring us some damn ranch dressing," I sigh at Leigh.

"Is that all you two want?" She grins at us.

"Better bring two orders," he holds up two fingers.

"You are such a bad influence," I scold him as she leaves.

"Only when it will benefit me. Haven't seen you in a minute, kiddo. What's going on?"

This is why I love my brother. He knows almost immediately that I need to talk, and he doesn't beat around the bush.

"Just busy, with Darren and everything," I grab a packet of sugar, opening it before putting it in my tea.

"Welcome to parenthood. It just gets busier, like you think things will level out, but they don't," he shakes his head. "Thank God Ruby is working with Whitney now, otherwise it would be harder, but you never really quit being a parent. You worry about shit, you swore to yourself you never would."

There's a worry I've had at the back of my mind for weeks. "Caleb, can I ask you a serious question."

"You know you can always ask me anything. Will I tell you what you want to hear? Not a chance, but I'll give you the best advice I can."

Those words warm my heart, he's never gone easy on me, and I don't want him to now. "Do you think I'm cut out for this with Darren and Nick?"

He takes a sip of his water, both of us lean back as our cheese fries are brought to the table. We look at each other, both waiting to see who will make the first move. In the end, it's me who can't wait, I lean in with a fork, grabbing a generous serving before dipping it in the ranch. Caleb chuckles as he does the same.

"I think you're more prepared than most people are, Kels. You've grown up so much in the last few years. You're responsible and loving, you care about others in a way not many do. You have a capacity to see the good, even when it would be easier to see the bad. You're who I want my kids to be like when they grow up. You're fulfilling your destiny right now," he grabs my hand, squeezing it tightly.

I sniff, brushing tears from below my eyes. "I didn't know you could be so sweet."

He laughs. "I got a rep to protect, don't let it get out."

Not being able to help it, I get up from my side of the booth, scoot in next to him and hug his neck tightly. "You're the best brother I could have ever asked for."

"It's always been my job to protect you, but now maybe it's your job to protect someone else."

Maybe, just maybe he's right.

TWENTY-TWO

Kelsea

I have the apartment to myself and it's magnificent. Not that I don't enjoy having the boys with me, but so quickly I turned into a caretaker. My showers are usually between five and ten minutes long. I never get to take a bath anymore.

That's about to change today. I'm off work, Nick's somewhere doing manly stuff with Ransom, and Darren's at school. The tub isn't huge in this bathroom, but it's big enough for me to lay down in. The room is steamy, just the way I like it.

Taking off my clothes, I dip down into the water, groaning as it caresses my tired muscles. The bubbles and bath oil I use, soak into my skin, relaxing in a way only they know how. Who knew taking care of a home with two other people in it would make me so tired? Tilting my head back against a rolled-up towel, I close my eyes.

I must doze off, because the next thing I hear is a sharp intake of breath that startles me. Glancing over at the door, I see Nick. He's wearing a pair of shorts, a tank top, sweaty and his laser gaze is right on me.

"Don't move," his voice is deep, sexy and just on this side of dangerous. "Am I in a fucking wet dream? You laying there all uncovered, looking at me with your sleepy gaze?"

I don't say anything, instead I let my gaze slip down to where he's pushing the palm of his hand against the bulge in his shorts. He stalks over to me, kneels down, reaches in. His big hand cups my breast, caressing as he moans deep in his throat. I groan along with him as he leans over, capturing the nub in his mouth, twirling his tongue around it, nipping with his teeth.

We've been ships, passing in the night for a few weeks now, neither one of us have been able to take time to do anything like this. My fingers rake at his tank top, wanting to feel his skin. Before I know what's happening, he's coming over the edge of the tub, clothes and all, laying his body over top of mine, spreading my thighs, making room for himself.

"Did you ever get on birth control, Kels?"

We're both pushing at his shorts. "Yeah, we can do this," I'm gasping, panting, wanting to feel him lose control with me.

I don't even know how it happens, the next thing I know, the water is being let out of the tub, the shower curtain has been pulled, and warm water rains over top of us. Right as Nick pushes inside of me. It's all a dreamy haze as his lips move all over my body, his hands are everywhere, and his strong cock is thrusting in, pulling out, pulsing against the pull of my core.

"Not gonna last long, Kels. I've wanted you every night as you lay next to me in bed."

"Agreed," I press up as he pushes down.

When his hand goes between us, his thumb pressing against my clit, I know I'm done for. Burying my face in his neck, I scream, wanting him to hear exactly how much he affects me.

"So close," he lunges. "So fuckin' close."

"Do it, Nick, do it for me," I encourage him, hitching my legs up higher, digging my fingers into his shoulders.

He doesn't stop, he presses harder, pushing me up against the tub, until I'm almost in a sitting position. His hands cup my ass, bringing me into full contact as he tries to get as deep as he can.

"You blow my mind," he puts his forehead on my shoulder and pistons his hips into mine.

The noises he makes, I'm not even sure what to call them, but the bounce off the walls in the room, turning me on more than I ever have before. His rhythm is jerky, fast, and with an abandonment I've never been taken with before. When I feel his cock lengthen, pulse, and then I feel the burst of warmth inside me, I come again, holding on tightly as he bites against my shoulder.

As we both lay there in the aftermath, he lifts his head, kissing me on my jawline.

"Hey girl, hey," he teases.

I throw my head back laughing loudly before I hug him tightly. "Welcome home."

"If that's the reception I get, I'm gonna go out more often."

Neither one of us move for a long time after that, both of us content to just be.

TWENTY-THREE

Nick

I'm running late as I clock in, but I can't wipe the smile off my face. Spending the time with Kels I got to this afternoon was much needed for both of us. I don't think anyone is going to be able to turn this smile upside down today.

"You riding tonight?" I ask Ransom as he comes in right behind me.

"Yeah, but I'm running late. Stella was having a rough time."

"Running late, too." I laugh as I point to the clock.

He looks at me, his eyebrows drawn in suspicion. "Funny, you don't look like you're even worried about running late."

"I had a great afternoon." I give him a shit-eating grin.

"I just fuckin' bet you did."

The one thing about having a best friend is you never fully have to explain anything to them. They know just by looking at you. He reaches out, giving me a handshake. "Get you some." He coughs as we see Mason walking out of the main office.

"What's going on with you two?" Menace asks. "Why aren't you already on the road?"

"Both running late, but we're getting out there now," I assure him.

He leaves while Ransom and I giggle like two boys caught with their hands in the cookie jar.

"See you for lunch?" he asks.

"Yeah, if it's not busy we'll grab something around midnight? Sound good for you?"

"See you then."

Walking out to where our patrol cars are parked, I get into mine, do my walkthrough, and get ready to ride the roads for the night.

IT'S BEEN A SLOW NIGHT, not many calls, hardly anyone speeding. It's looking like it might be one of those easy shifts that we sometimes get. I'm making rounds through the county. If anyone were to ask me, this would be my absolute favorite thing. When I just got to drive around, looking for people who might be up to no good.

Driving down one of the main thoroughfares, I see some metal laying in the street. Knowing someone will drive by, not paying attention, I pull my squad car over, turn my lights on, and start dragging it out of the way of oncoming traffic.

Almost every person who works in law enforcement will tell you there's a certain feeling you get when shit's about to go down. It's a sinking of your gut, a chill to your skin and bones, a prickling to the back of your neck. Right now I'm feeling this more than I've ever felt it. The bad thing? I'm out in the open and I don't know which way the danger is coming from. It could be both or either.

A shot rings out from in front of me. The spark of the gun shines brightly, outlining a truck sitting a few feet up. It's so dark out here, that I hadn't noticed it before.

Firing at the person, I try to get back behind my car, use it for a little bit of cover, but the person starts running toward me. "Put your hands up! I will fire!" I put some authority in my voice.

The person comes into the beam of my headlights, and I see the person is Ezra. "Ezra!" I scream, knowing my body cam will catch what I've said. "Put the gun down!"

He shoots again, hitting me in the side, right as I reach my patrol car and wrench the door open. I crouch behind it, emptying my clip, hoping like hell I've gotten him enough so that he won't come back for more.

When I try to stand, I realize I'm dizzy, there's blood pouring from my side and I know I'm in deep shit.

Reaching for my radio in the car, I feel it in my hand right as the world goes black.

TWENTY-FOUR

Kelsea

"Thanks for coming out with me tonight." I glance over at Stella. "I know you're tired and you didn't really feel like it, so thank you."

Darren had ended up asking to stay at my brother's for dinner, which allowed me to have a girls' night.

"You know I'm always up to have a good time with you, Kels. Even if sometimes I'm not feeling great, don't ever think you can't ask me to come out with you. Speaking of, I can't believe you and Nick haven't decided to put a name on whatever it is you two have. I'd like to kick his ass," she growls as she comes to a stop sign. "If he doesn't know what he has with you, he's a dumbass."

"Trust me," I laugh. "I wanna kick his ass too, but I have to believe he'll get a wake-up call. I mean, if we end up being able to adopt Darren, we'll have to deal with each other for the rest of our lives." For some reason I almost cry at the thought.

"I have every faith that one day you'll be like me and Ransom. A couple of newlyweds who feel like we've been married for ten years, expecting our first kid."

I watch as she reaches down, cupping her baby bump, as she drives toward what is now mine and Nick's apartment. Sighing heavily, I watch the passing scenery as we drive by. "I hope you're right."

"You know I'm always right!"

I giggle loudly. "Whatever you say, Stelle. Whatever you say."

Up ahead we see the flashing lights of a Laurel Springs Police Car, but what's odd, is they don't have anyone pulled over in front of them. It's facing our direction, dread fills my stomach as we get closer. The driver's side door is open, and the siren is still blaring. "Definitely not Ransom, since it's not a SUV," Stelle says as she slows down.

As she creeps by, I see booted feet laying underneath the edge of the door. "Stelle, stop, they're down. Whoever they are, they're down."

Before her car comes to a complete stop, I've unbuckled and I'm out of the passenger seat, running around the front. In my periphery I can see her put on her flashers, and then her door is opening, as she gets out. "Who is it?"

Every bit of the food I've just eaten for dinner threatens to come back up as I see the love of my life, the man whose helping me raise a child laying there. His skin is pale, his arm outstretched for the radio in his patrol car. There's blood pooling under his neck, and my heart pounds heavily as I hit the concrete beside him. "It's Nick," I manage to push the words out from between my dry lips. I immediately start to look and see where he's bleeding from. Blood coats my hands and I look up at her. Our eyes meet and an unspoken conversation happens between us. We're both scared to death, but we suck it up, and do what we do best. "It's Nick."

"Let me see." She pushes me away, and I let her. She's the registered nurse with more training than I have. In the car the radio is going off, questioning where Nick is.

I've been in enough police cars to know how to work a few things inside. My hands shake as I turn the siren off, then reach for the radio. Blood makes it slip through my grip first. "Fuck, please God, please God." My bottom lip trembles and I do my best to control my breathing. Going through everything I've seen my brother and my dad do, I reach forward to the radio, hitting a button. When nothing happens, I hit it again.

"Dispatch." I hear through the radio.

It's then that it dawns on me I have to speak. My hands tremble as I bring the microphone up to my lips. I hit the button again, before I whisper. "Officer down, officer down."

"Come again? I can't understand you."

Clearing my throat, I go again, letting the hysteria take hold of me. "Janet. It's Kelsea – Mason's daughter and Caleb's sister – there's an officer down! Nick's been shot. We found him on our way home."

"Where are you, Kelsea?" she asks quickly.

"Umm." I look around, checking for street signs, but I can't see anything.

"Pull it together, Kelsea. Where are you?" she asks again.

"I don't know the name of the street, but we passed the Methodist Church. We went through the stop sign, coming from The Café. We haven't made it to the bottoms yet," I push forward in an excited utterance.

"I'm gonna get help to you. Stay off the radio unless you need to report a change in his condition. You'll have a cavalry in just a minute."

Inhaling deeply to keep myself from throwing up, I listen intently to what she says next. Sobbing as I hear her voice.

"Gunshot wound, gunshot wound. Officer down, officer down between Spring St. and the bottoms, right past the Methodist Church."

Throwing the radio into the passenger seat, I climb out, getting back down on the ground next to Stella. "Has he come to?"

"No." I can hear the tears in her voice. "I'm trying to see where he was hit, but I don't wanna move him."

Reaching into my pocket, I grab my cell out, turning the flashlight on. "Here, let's look."

As I feel along the edges of his vest, he makes an anguished sound. "Nick? Nick? Can you hear me?"

Those eyes of his open slightly, but I hate the paleness of his face. "Kels?"

"I'm here," I sob quietly. "I'm right here, what do you need?"

"My dash cam and my body cam, make sure it's secured. I got Ezra on there," he croaks out as he takes a breath that I can hear gurgle in his throat.

"Where are you hit?" I don't bother to wipe the tears off my face as I look down at the man I love so damn much.

"My side hurts," he groans as he points to the side I'm kneeling on.

Stella takes the cell phone out of my hand and shines it where he indicated. "Shit, he got you where you have a gap in your vest."

"Stay with me," I tell him, as I see his eyes start to close. "Stay with me. We're here with you, just stay with me," I beg him. "We've got so much to do." The words barely make it out. "A child, a relationship to figure the fuck out, a life to build, Nick. Stay with me, please."

Stella continues working on him as I keep my gaze pinned to his.

"I'm sorry Kels, I'm so fuckin' sorry that I've not let you in."

"Stop." I put my fingers to his lips. "Stop, save your strength. We'll figure this out somewhere besides the side of the road."

"We may not have that time." His voice is insistent. "Tell Mom and Dad I love them. Love hasn't been," – he breathes deeply again, the sound rattling around in his chest – "an easy thing for me to do." He coughs. I grip his hand tightly in mine. "But I love you." I see tears leaking out of the corners of his eyes. "I do. If I've ever loved anybody, it's been you."

I'm losing my mind as I sit here, holding his hand, listening to him talk. "I love you too, but you don't have to tell me all of this. We've got time."

"No, we don't," he argues. "Stella, thank you for being the best sister I could have ever asked for. I love you more than I could say. You've always understood everything without me having to say a word. The connection we've had since the day I came to live with you has been everything I could have asked for."

"I love you too, Nick," Stella cries. "Now please stop talking. Save your strength."

"I just..." he exhales. "Just wanted you all to know."

As his head tilts to the side, the paramedics and other members of the Laurel Springs PD arrive. Both Stella and I are pushed away as Morgan and Blaze work on him.

"He's not flat-lining," Blaze assures us. "He passed out from blood loss, but we've got to get him out of here. What do you all need?" She glances at Ransom who looks like he's about to lose it himself.

"His body cam," he answers, the words strangled. "It's on his vest."

"It was Ezra," I blurt. "He told me when he still had a little energy left."

"Get it quick, and let us do what we need," she tells him as she steps back.

"Got it." But I notice he takes a moment to grip Nick's hand, giving his best friend all the strength he can. "We'll meet you at the hospital."

"C'mon." I hear at my back. "I'll take you over."

The one person I want besides Nick is right there holding me up. When I look up into the face I love so much, I officially break down. "Daddy..." I throw myself at him, letting his strong arms catch me. "Please tell me he's not going to die," I wail into his shirt and vest, letting the tears flow, letting the sobs out.

He pulls me away from him. "Nick is one of the strongest men I know. He's gonna flight, Kels. Y'all are gonna figure this shit out, and we're gonna get the fucker who shot him and left him for dead on the side of the road like a dog."

"Damn right we are." I hear my brother, who holds his hand out for the body cam. "Y'all go ahead. Ace and I are on this. Keep us apprised, but we're gonna get this son of a bitch tonight if we can."

It's a blur as I'm herded to my Dad's car, buckled in and sitting next to the man who always makes me feel safe. It's then I know I have to come clean, someone else has to know this secret besides Stella.

"Dad." I reach over, grabbing his hand with mine. He grips it tightly. "I'm in love with Nick," I sob, coughing as I sniffle, trying to keep it together. "And he might die tonight. How do I handle this?"

"Oh Kels." He returns my tight grip. "Let's get through the next few hours and then we can talk about it."

"Okay," I nod, agreeing because I don't know what else to do.

"Just take a deep breath, sweetheart. We'll get this figured out."

I do what I've done for most of my life. I let my dad take my fear, and I do my best to believe that only good will prevail.

TWENTY-FIVE

Mason (Menace)

It's hard to watch my daughter fall apart in front of me, and even harder to watch the Keplers try and keep their heads about them as we all gather at the hospital in Birmingham The last time we were all here was when Ransom got shot, and I don't think any of us have forgotten that.

Kelsea looks like a ghost of herself. She's always been my bright, vibrant girl who took after her mom. There's no room she can't light up, but right now her light is gone. It's a reminder of what destruction the world can bring, even when it looks like you've got the world in the palm of your hands.

I'm furious this happened to Nick as he was doing his job. As he was protecting the people of Laurel Springs. It makes me angry someone would come gunning for him because he was trying to protect a boy from a father who's much more like a predator.

"Thank you so much for keeping him." I can hear her saying to Ruby. "Please don't turn the TV on. He doesn't know, and I don't want him to know yet. I'd like to be the one to tell him. Love you."

"Renegade and Havoc are headed out to keep him safe," I tell her. "Caleb and Ace are already tracking Ezra down. They will get him." Maybe me being so positive about it to her will make me feel more confident about it, too.

"I just don't understand," Whitney cries. "How did they get him from the highway? How could he not have seen?"

Ransom, more pissed than I've ever seen him, answers the question. "Because he was fucking ambushed. He never even saw Ezra coming. I saw the bodycam footage. He was dragging shit out of the middle of the road, trying to make it safe for the public and he was fucking shot. Please tell me Caleb and Ace have found him."

"They're trying." I put my hand on his shoulder, squeezing reassuringly.

"They better not stop until they get him."

Stella puts her arms around Ransom's waist. "I'm sure they're doing the best they can, handsome. Be patient."

"It's hard to be patient when my best friend is in surgery."

"Think about how I felt." She rubs his chest. "Knowing you were back there and I couldn't do anything to help. Imagine how he felt. We just have to be willing to let the doctor's work."

My eyes shift over to where Kelsea sits with her back to the wall. She's got her cell phone in her hand.

"What's going on?" I ask as I have a seat next to her.

"He'd texted me earlier, asking if I wanted to go to the lake this weekend, and I didn't answer him," she cries, rubbing her cheeks. "I thought I would be able to talk to him when he got home, and this, she shows me an obviously personal picture of theirs. He's got a smile on his face that I've never seen him have. It's obvious he cares deeply for my daughter.

"We took this the other day," she sniffs. "When we were

waiting to get a banana split at The Café with Darren. We realized we didn't have many pictures together. We took a family one, and then Nick and I took this one."

"You both look so happy."

She glances up at me, her eyes wet. "We were, so much happier than I've ever been. I keep wondering if maybe this happened because we were happy. Like maybe people aren't allowed to have things work out like you dreamed they would. Because I dreamed of this life with him, Dad." She wipes under her eyes. "Even when he was so closed off I couldn't even get a smile out of him, I dreamed of a life like this with him."

I hug her tightly. "I know you did, and he loves you, he's going to fight for you."

She sniffles again, breaking every piece of my heart. "I hope so."

Stella

Common sense tells me I shouldn't be here, I should be keeping my stress level down. My heart says there's nowhere else I want to be. Ransom sits down. Calmer now, he puts his arm around my neck, holding me close.

"He's gonna be okay, ya know that, right? He's a stubborn son of a bitch."

Tears streak down my face. "I know, I keep thinking back to that summer he wrecked the four-wheeler. Remember that?" I smile.

There's an answering smile on Ransom's face. Not wanting to be in the here and now, I let my mind drift back a few years.

"How bad is it?" I stand with my hands on my hips, looking at my new brother. I haven't really called him that yet, but he officially took my last name two weeks ago.

"Not bad." He grimaces as he tries to get off the four-wheeler.

"Liar, you can barely get off the dang thing. We need to go tell mom and dad."

"No!" he argues.

"What if it's broken?" I argue back.

"It ain't like it's the first time I ever had a broken bone, Stella. It'll just be the first time it didn't come from the end of another person's fist."

I'm quiet as I think about what he's said, and it breaks my heart. "But if it's broken, you'll need to go to the hospital."

"Never have before." He turns away from me, like he thinks this argument is over.

"Dude, if I were you, I'd just listen to her," Ransom echoes from up ahead where he's stopped his four-wheeler. "She gets something in her head, and she doesn't let it go."

"Thank you, I think." I make a face at Ransom.

Turning back to Nick, I try again. "Let me just call them and see what we should do." I point to a gas station up the road. "They'll let us use a phone since our cells don't have signal out here."

"No!" he yells.

"Why not? If you're hurt, you should be seen!" I yell back.

Neither Ransom nor I expect the sound that comes from Nick's chest, it's like the war cry of a wounded animal. His face is red, his chest pumping up and down.

"I don't want to give them a reason to send me away." His voice is at a whisper as he finishes the statement. "I like it here, I like it with your family. I don't want to move again."

Walking over to him, I take his very broken arm in my hands. "Who says you'll have to leave? It's not my family, it's our family. Your last name is Kepler, and there's nothing that's ever going to change that. Got it?"

He looks like he wants to argue, but I do what I do best, and that's bulldoze right over a situation. Within the next fifteen minutes, we've called my parents and they're on their way to take Nick to the Emergency Room.

"Besides," – I hit his shoulder with mine as we sit together, waiting on them to show up – "you'll get a badass cast that everyone can sign, and you can make up how you hurt yourself. Ya know, seem really cool for all the girls."

He blushes, laughing along with me. "I've never had a sister before."

"I've never had a brother before either, but I think if I were ever given the option to choose one, it would have been you."

Ransom grins at me. "We didn't get to ride four-wheelers the whole rest of that summer, but I can remember going to Six Flags, and they let us in the front of every line because he had a cast. He thought he was hot shit."

"We all did," I remind him, putting my hands on my stomach. "We even got free food out of it."

My laughter fades into tears.

"Babe, what's wrong?" he asks, cupping my cheeks, those serious eyes of his searching mine.

"What if he's not here for this baby? What if I have to do this without him?"

"Don't even think like that." Ransom hugs me tightly. "Remember the story of your mom being pregnant with you and Trevor getting hurt? This shit has come full circle. Things will be fine."

As I look up at the patient board, the display telling me that Nick is still in surgery, I hope Ransom's right. I can't do any of this without the boy who means so much to me.

TWENTY-SIX

Caleb

If I could legally kill this son of a bitch, I would do it. I've watched the footage from Nick's body cam twice now. Both times I've fought not to puke. This man has no regard for human life, and those are the miserable pricks that deserve to spend their lives behind bars.

They don't get to have the love of a woman, the warmth of a bed, the freedom to move about as they would like to, and to be honest they don't fucking deserve it. As I hear Nick grunt when he gets hit by the bullet, I feel sick again.

"I can't watch this shit anymore, I'm ready to kill this motherfucker."

Ace clears his throat as he secures his bulletproof vest, then puts a jacket over it, proclaiming he's a member of the Laurel Springs Police Department. Looking at him, I know he's just as ready to put an end to this as I am. "Where we going first?"

"Dumbass like him? He'd go straight home."

"You think so?"

I nod, securing my vest, making sure my side arm is ready to go. "He won't have anyone to run to. Chances are because he kept Darren isolated, he's also kept himself isolated. None of us know what we're facing though, that means he's had plenty of time to load up. SWAT will back us up," I tell him. "But I want him. When we take him down, I want to cuff this bastard. I've never seen my sister so upset, and this asshole is going to take the blame for that."

Minutes later, we're flying down the streets of Laurel Springs. Ace drives, because I don't have it in me to not act like a fool just so we can get there faster. Part of me wanted to argue with him, the other part of me knew it would be better for me to sit here and stew.

"Ya know." Ace slows to take a turn, accelerating as we come out of the curve. "When Ryan and Whitney first talked about taking a foster child, I thought they were insane. It's weird, but up until that point in my life, I thought all foster kids were inherently bad with chips on their shoulders."

"I think we all kinda did, but Ruby offered to tutor him, and we got to know him better. He was smart as hell and all he needed to be given was a chance to succeed."

"He grew up to be a damn good man," Ace agrees.

"And for him to be ambushed like that?" I hit my fist against the dashboard. "Pisses me the fuck off."

SWAT HAS ARRIVED, along with over half of the Laurel Springs Police Department. Grabbing the microphone for our outdoor system, I take a deep breath and call him out.

"Ezra Metcalfe, you're surrounded! Come out with your hands up!"

All of us are prepared for the bullets that buzz by our

heads. Going for a bit more cover, I say the same words again. This time we're shot at, but I distinctly hear a *fuck you*!

"He won't come out." Ace looks at me. "He's gonna make us go in there and get his ass."

"Should we breach?" the SWAT commander questions.

"I don't think so, we don't know what he's got in there. Maybe we draw him out? If we wait, he'll probably come out on his own."

Ace's eyes get wide as he points his gun toward the house. "Or maybe he comes out with guns pointed at us."

I turn, looking to where Ace's gaze is fixed. There are a number of people telling Ezra to drop his weapon, and when he fails to do so, deadly measures are taken.

"Fuckin' waste." I punch my vest because it's just all so damn unnecessary. "Call it in."

Kelsea

"It was suicide by cop," Caleb tells me. "He gave us no choice but to shoot him, and I say that as a person who really wanted to watch him pay for what he did to Nick."

Regardless of who this man is, Darren's now lost the only flesh and blood he's ever known. "Can you bring Darren to me?"

"Yeah." He sighs heavily into the phone. "He's asleep but I'll grab him and drive down there. All of this should come from you since he's comfortable with you."

"Thanks." I disconnect the call, wrapping my arms around my waist. How the fuck am I going to do this? How am I going to tell Darren his father tried to kill Nick and now his father is dead?

Arms wrap around me and I rest my head on my mom's shoulder. "I don't think I'm strong enough for this, Mom."

"You are, you're a Harrison through and through. We rise to occasions like this."

"It's just so senseless, I want to scream, cry, and beat anything that'll let me get this damn aggression out. It didn't have to be like this. It's so unfair."

"Life isn't fair." She hugs me tighter. "If there's one thing I hope I've taught you, it's that. But just because it's not fair doesn't mean you have to stoop to their level. You can handle this with your head held high."

"How? All I want to do right now is crawl in a hole and never come out."

"You do that, Kels? And they win."

She turns me around to face her. "You go in that bathroom, compose yourself, and fix your face. You're the one person he'll want to see when he gets here, and you have to pull it together, baby girl. Once you get through telling him, we'll sit together and pray as a family, because that's what we are."

All I want to do right now is curl up in a ball and never face the world again, but I know my mom is right.

"KELS!" I hear his voice before I see his body running toward me. I catch Darren in a hug, squeezing him tighter than I've ever squeezed anyone else. "What's happening?"

I know he's probably heard other people talk, and I know it's up to me to be the one whose honest with him, the one he can ask questions of, the one who can wipe his tears if he has them. Taking him to the edge of the waiting area, I sit him down, then turn to face him.

"Nick got shot tonight."

"By my dad?" he asks quietly, his eyes wide.

There's no point in lying to him. "Yes, by your dad, and I

have some information about your dad. When they went to arrest him, he tried to shoot the cops. They ended up shooting him."

I pause, because I'm not sure if I'm doing this right.

"So he'll never hurt me again?" he asks.

"Never again."

He lets loose a long breath, his shoulders seem to slump from what appears to be a huge weight he's been carrying. "I love him, but I hate him too. He made me scared of him. I like you and Nick better. I feel loved with you two."

Wrapping my arms around him, I kiss him on the forehead. "Then with us is where you'll be. Wanna say a prayer with me for your dad and Nick?"

He nods, slipping his small hand in mine. As we bow our heads, I have a silent prayer of my own, one hoping I'm doing the right thing.

TWENTY-SEVEN

Kelsea

Waiting is the worst, especially as Darren sits curled up next to me. I have to admit, even though I'm sad about the events that brought him here, I'm happy to have him beside me. For the last few weeks, he's been my buddy. While I would do anything to take away the pain I know he's feeling, I'm almost glad he doesn't have to grow up with the piece of shit father he had.

Sighing, I look at my watch, wondering how long it's going to be before someone comes out and tells us how he's doing. He went into recovery almost an hour ago, according to the patient board. I'm about to not be patient any longer.

"Do you want some coffee, honey?" I look up, seeing Whitney.

"I should be asking you, if you need anything." I scoot over, doing my best not to disturb Darren.

"No." She grabs hold of my hand. "He'd want me to take care of you."

For some reason Whitney saying those words starts the

water works I've been trying to hold at bay for the last three hours since Darren showed up. She puts her arm around my shoulder, hugging me tightly.

"He loves you, you know that, right?"

My chin trembles as I try to keep my emotions in check. "I know he does, he just has a hard time expressing his feelings."

"He does," she agrees. "Did you ever hear how he came to live with us?" She asks as Darren shifts off me in his sleep.

"No." I shake my head. I've only heard parts of the story here and there. No one has ever told me the whole thing.

"C'mon, let's take a walk."

I don't want to leave this place, because they might get an update, and then I won't be around. She must notice the panic in my face as she holds up what looks like a beeper. "They'll let us know when he's awake."

"And I'll take care of Darren," Mom says as she comes to sit next to him, smoothing his hair back softly.

Walking next to Whitney is soothing, I'm not exactly sure why or how, maybe it's because we both love Nick and we have that common bond.

"It all started when Ryan came home from work one day. He was furious and bothered by something he'd seen when he was working a theft case. He told me about the teenage boy who'd stolen food because he was hungry and clothes because his clothes were too small. He'd left an IOU in place of everything he'd stolen." She wipes at her eyes. "Even when the world has tried to push him down, Nick's always been a stand-up person."

"He has." I think back to things I've seen him do, how he holds me at night when he doesn't think I'm paying attention.

"So anyway, Ryan comes home with this story of this teenager, and I don't know." she shrugs. "Something came over me, and I asked him if he had anyone to take care of him."

"That sounds like something you would do." I grin at her.

"We tried to have another one after Stella, but it never worked out for us, and the moment he mentioned Nick, I knew I was waiting for him. We were supposed to have him. He needed a home full of love, we had one. The very next day I went to a lawyer friend of ours, and Ryan went to some people who owed him a few favors. Within a week he was in our home. Within a week, he was *ours*," she emphasizes the word. "And we've never looked back."

I ask the one question I'm always wanted to know. "How did Stella react? I know how she told me she reacted, but I've always wondered if she did or not."

"It was weird, they immediately started fighting like brother and sister. They had these little inside jokes within a day, and it was like they'd grown up together. Ryan and I were half-way scared, what were we in for? Stella was a bit of a handful, and now we're adding someone who seems like he's going to be her best buddy? There were a lot of sleepless nights when they were teenagers. Who am I kidding? I still have sleepless nights, especially if Nick doesn't text me when he gets off work, and sometimes he forgets."

"I'll make sure he does it from now on," I assure her, because I know how I would feel if I were waiting up, wanting to make sure he was safe. This woman beside me has probably had thousands of sleepless nights.

"Thanks Kelsea, but really all I want you to do is make Nick happy, and I think you do."

"I think so too." I lift my shoulder up. "But it's so hard to tell with him."

Footsteps beat against the hallway, causing us to look up.

"He's awake!" Ransom yells. "And he's asking for you, Kels."

IF ANYONE HAD ASKED me before this moment if I had any that were incredibly important to me so far in this life, I'd probably have listed off a small handful. That is, until this one.

Until the moment I walk into Nick's hospital room and see him awake and alive.

"Is that my blood?" he asks first as he reaches out for my hand.

I completely forgot it was just a few hours ago that Stella and I had worked on saving him. "It is, Stella and I found you."

"I thought so." His voice is hoarse, probably from the tube they put down it, and the surgery. "I wasn't sure if I had dreamed you two or not."

"No, we were there."

"Then I told you?" He grips my hand in his, entwining our fingers together.

"It's late and this has been a crazy day, so please forgive me, but told me what?"

"That if I could love anyone it would be you?"

My breath catches in my throat as I look into the dark eyes of the man I love. "You did."

He closes his eyes. "I was wrong, I was so wrong, Kels. I saw the other side tonight and I don't like what I saw. I promised myself if I got to speak to you again, if I was just given one more shot, I wouldn't blow it."

Tears are streaming down my face. "You never blew anything. I'm always gonna be here for you."

"I did blow it." He holds my hand tighter. "You've been here for me, for years, and I've just taken it for granted, never let you know how I feel, never did anything that would put me out there. You've always been the vulnerable one, Kels. Well this is it. I fuckin' love the shit outta you. You make my life brighter, you make my days happier, and you give me purpose. Please tell me I haven't fucked up."

Leaning down so that I can kiss his dry lips, I know my tears are leaking onto his face, but right now I don't care.

"I love you too, Nick Kepler, and you're never gonna get rid of me."

He laughs hoarsely. "Good, because I don't ever want you to go anywhere."

As I lift up, the door opens and in runs Darren. "Nick! Are you okay?"

"I'm fine, takes more than a bullet to put me out of commission."

"My dad's dead." He says the words so matter-of-factly. "But I'm okay because I'm with you and he can't hurt me anymore."

Nick looks to me for confirmation and when I nod, he let's go of me to wrap Darren up in his arms. "You're damn right about that. You're gonna be with us, and nobody else will hurt you anymore."

I know with everything I am that's a promise both of us will keep.

TWENTY-EIGHT

Nick

If the bullet that hit me didn't kill me, physical therapy sure as hell will. The therapist they've given me is sadistic. Now I know why Ransom was such a little bitch when he was rehabbing. I might owe him an apology or two.

"Come on, Nick, one more set," she encourages me in this all too peppy voice. "I know you have one more in you."

I want to tell her to shut the fuck up, but at the same time, I'm struggling with not being on the job. I badly want to be back in my squad car, riding the roads and taking lunch with Ransom. If I ever want to be allowed to do that again, she has to sign off on it.

When I have absolutely nothing else left to give, she claps her hands. "That's it for today, Nick."

I'm breathing heavily, wishing it didn't take so much out of me to do PT, but it does. I'm so weak compared to where I was a few months ago, but I'm also better than I was a few weeks ago. "See you in a few days." I wave as I use a towel to dry off my wet hair.

Walking into the heat of the Alabama afternoon, I almost want to go back in and do another round of PT. Luckily, I see Ransom at the patient pickup. Waving over, I lightly jogg to where he's parked.

"Thanks for coming and getting me."

"No problem." He hands me a bottle of water. "Looks like you could use this."

"Dude, I'm tellin' you she likes to see me sweat."

There's a bark from the extended cab, and I glance back, seeing Rambo. "Hey, bub." I reach back to give him scratches on his ears. "You excited to be out with us today?" His tail wags back and forth, full of excitement.

"Darren's gonna love sitting back there with him." Ransom turns to the right, taking us to the elementary school. "Does he know you're picking him up today?"

"Yeah, I explained to him last night what's happening and warned him about not telling Kels. He knows this is a secret mission. Pull up here." I point to a spot for parents who are going to get their kids are instructed to park. "I'll be out in a few with him."

"Take your time, I ain't got shit to do today."

"RAMBO!" Darren squeals as he gets in the truck and Rambo starts licking his face.

"Leave it!" Ransom instructs with some bass in his voice. It always amazes me how this dog pays attention.

Rambo listens, putting his head in Darren's lap, while Darren buckles in and then strokes his head and scratches behind his ears.

"So where are we heading?" Ransom asks as he turns onto main street.

"Laurel Springs Bank and Trust. What I want is the family lockbox."

"Can I tell you how awesome this is?" Ransom grins like a fool. "No one else I know has a family lockbox. That's like southern royalty shit."

"Jesus dude, I bet your family has one, and if they don't, they should. It's home safety 101, don't keep things in your home that robbers could steal. You are a cop, right?"

"Shut up," he says as we pull into the bank parking lot.

"You wanna come in and see what a lockbox looks like?" I tease him.

"I know what the fuck it looks like."

"Hey." I point back to where Darren sits.

"I've heard worse."

Ransom laughs. "He's heard worse."

"While I'm sure he has, you're having your own kid in a few months and you should probably clean up the language."

"And you should probably take the stick out of your ass," he fires back.

I laugh, I can't help it, I bend over I'm laughing so hard. He laughs along with me.

"I'm glad you're here." He hitches his chin at me.

"I'm glad I am too."

As we walk into the bank, Ransom asks the question I've been waiting for him to ask all day. "What are we getting out of this lockbox?"

"An engagement ring." I grin at Darren as I say those words.

Ransom looks back and forth between the both us, while we grin. "Well I'll be damned," he laughs. "My little boy done went and joined us big boys."

"I would normally say fuck you to that, but it's the truth. I finally became a man. One who can tell the woman I love I love her, and one who can put a ring on her finger. I'm proud of where I've been and now where I am. Yeah, I have grown up."

And nothing else has ever felt so right.

Kelsea

I haven't gotten my hair done in forever. Maybe it's because I've been taking better care of Nick than I have myself, but I'm super excited to be hanging out with Stella and Ruby today.

When I walk in, I see them both already sitting in chairs. "C'mon over here, Kels," my hair girl, Tiffany says as she points to me. "What are we doing today?"

"Cutting this length off." I blow my bangs out of my eyes. "And maybe some highlights?"

"Sounds good." She goes to work, while I get settled.

"How's it going with Nick?" Stella asks as she rubs her stomach. I've noticed her doing it more and more since she got a bigger bump.

"He's doing well. He hates physical therapy and he can't drive yet, but Ransom is chauffeuring him around today. He can deal with his bad attitude after PT," I joke.

"Is he that bad?" Ruby asks as she takes a drink from her can of Coke.

"It depends on what kind of a day he's had. Like I can't blame him, it's got to be super hard for him, but at some point it's going to get easier, ya know? He just wants to be back in his squad car, and while I get it, it makes it difficult to live with him at times."

"Has he at least been cleared for the physical stuff?" Stella giggles.

"Look lady, just because you're in your horny trimester of

pregnancy, doesn't mean the rest of us are. But to answer your question, yes he was and we had a good time trying to stay quiet so we wouldn't wake Darren up. So there." I maturely stick out my tongue at her.

"Girl, I know where that tongue's probably been." She throws a magazine at me. "Put it back in your mouth."

The three of us giggle like schoolgirls. I've missed this, and I'm so glad I'm getting the chance to hang out with my friends today.

TWENTY-NINE

Nick

"You're sure it's okay for him to stay tonight?"

My mom grins as she takes hold of Darren's hand, welcoming him into their home. "It's more than okay. We're gonna have so much fun, you and Kels have a great time."

We've never left him alone for the whole night, but after the last few months, we kinda feel like we deserve a night out. I go back to work in three weeks, and I know better than anyone how much time I'll have to be putting in. Everyone has covered for me while I've been away, and I'll only want to put in that same time for my coworkers.

"Be good for them," I kneel down. "If you get scared or anything, you can call either one of us, I promise. We'll come to get you."

On the way over, he'd confided in me he'd never spent the night with anyone before like this.

He nods. "Okay."

"He'll be fine," Dad says as he comes into the living room, covered in saw dust. "I'm gonna show him my shop."

"You're in for a treat D-man, he showed me his shop when I was about fifteen, so you're gonna get a hell of a jump on my skills."

He looks interested, and eventually dad lures him out with the promise of it being man's work. I wave to mom as I leave, thanking her again for taking care of him.

"It's my pleasure. You and Kels have a great time."

That's exactly what we plan to do.

"WHERE ARE WE GOING?" She asks as I hit the interstate heading south.

"We're going to Birmingham. I've got a surprise for you," I smile over at her. "You've done so much for me, with taking on Darren, taking me on. I want to give you a little something in return."

The smile she gives me lights up her whole face. "Is this why you told me to dress nice?" She indicates the little black dress she's wearing.

"Yeah," I turn from her, focusing on the traffic as we make the drive. "I wanted to give you a nice night, you deserve it."

"So do you," she reaches over, grabbing my hand.

Looking down at our clasped hands on the console, I can't help but imagine this will last forever. Like we do the whole thing. Marriage, maybe more kids. It's the first time I've ever imagined it with anyone, and it feels right.

"You know, I had never been to Birmingham until I moved into Mom and Dad's house."

"Really?" She asks, curling towards me with her body.

Talking with her is easier than I thought it would be, but it's still difficult. "Yeah, like never on a vacation, never really outside of Laurel Springs. I remember us driving down sixty-five, and seeing the big buildings pop out of nowhere. There's a Popeye's a few exits before you get there."

She giggles. "I know which one you're talking about."

"We stopped there on the way back, and since then I've always had an affinity for Popeye's. But I remember being so amazed. There was a Starbuck's, Whataburger, and a Target, all at the same exit. It blew my mind. While all of that scared me slightly, I also wanted to experience it."

"It sounds like sensory overload."

"It was kind of, but I got my first froo froo coffee, my first Popeye's, and my first Whataburger all in the same day."

"Epic day for you," she deadpans.

"It was," I argue.

We look at each other, laughing at our argument. The GPS on the dash indicates I need to take the next exit. She's quiet as I follow the directions through downtown.

"Nick," she gasps. "Really? Flemings?"

"Yeah."

"Can we afford this?" She squeals slightly.

Leaning over, I push her hair back from her face, tucking it behind her ear. For once I don't stop the words that want to come. "I can afford anything to make you happy and to let you know that I appreciate you, Kels. Anything."

She turns her lips into my hand, kissing me softly on the palm. "I'm excited!"

The truth is so am I. *I love you, Kels.* Even if I can't say it out loud yet, I'll tell her every day in my mind.

THIRTY

Nick

As I pull my patrol car up to the house, I glance down at the time. This is my first day back on duty, and I know there's something I have to do. This house? It's held me back in so many ways. Each time I would move forward, it would pull me back, not allowing me to be the man I wanted to be.

Getting out, I slowly walk up to the front door, knocking twice before stepping back and waiting for someone to answer. When a woman with a small baby in her arms comes to the door, I give her my best smile.

"Hi, I'm Nick..."

"Cooper," she finishes. "You used to live here. I'm Colleen, I used to live over there." She points to another house farther down the block.

I vaguely remember her riding her bike with me when she was younger. "I remember."

"Yeah." She smiles this time a little sad. "My son and I, we moved here after he was born. Divorce," she says quietly.

"I'm not here to judge anyone, I was just wondering if I could look at my old room."

Anyone else except her would probably question my sanity, but she gets it. Stepping back from the door, she sweeps her arm out to the side. "Be my guest. There's not much in it now."

"No big deal."

As I approach the room where I spent some of my worst days, my palms sweat, my heart feels like it's about to beat out of my chest. But I know I have to let this house, this past go before I ask Kels to marry me. When I get to the door, I stop, closing my eyes. I can hear all my mom's old boyfriends and my stepdad screaming at me, telling me I'm not their kid so they don't have to worry about me.

Pushing the door open, it's like I'm taken back to another lifetime. There's still a chip in the plaster where my head hit it one night when my stepdad and I got into argument. There's a hole behind the door, where he shoved it open so forcefully it swung into the wall.

There's still a stain on the carpet where I pissed in fear. There's another stain where I lay, with my lip bleeding, hoping someone would take me away from here.

I would pray and bargain and pray again that someone would take me away and show me what real love was. Funny thing is I kept myself from believing it for all these years, because I've been scared of it. I've been scared of the one thing I wanted.

For so many years, love for me equaled hurt, and for me to fully accept the love that others want to give me, I know I've got to put teenage Nick to bed. He's got to be able to forgive not only the people who kicked his ass, but himself.

"You were just a kid," I tell myself. "You didn't know how to get out of the situation you were dropped into. It's time, time that you forget all the bullshit and live the happy life you have now. It's okay to let it all go."

Closing my eyes, I let all the memories flow through me, and surprisingly there's new ones. My mom bandaging up my knee as a kid, kissing the bandage, back when she looked healthy, before she went downhill. Us eating dinner together, laughing as we had ice cream sundaes. In that moment, I realize my mom wasn't a bad woman, she didn't know how to process her feelings, how to accept disappointment, love, anything. And if I don't change, if I don't break the cycle, I'll be right back in the place I've been for most of my life.

Taking a deep breath, I touch the wall, the one that had closed me in so tightly.

"I forgive you."

I whisper those words, chanting them until I feel it. In this room, Nick Cooper will die, and Nick Kepler will be the man he's always supposed to be. Because the Kepler last name? It breaks cycles.

As I leave a little later, I do so with a smile on my face and a lightness in my heart.

EPILOGUE ONE

Kelsea

"What are we doing out here?"

We're in the truck, enjoying some time to ourselves. I thought we were going to breakfast, but he's driving to his shop, it looks like. My gaze lingers on the console, where our fingers are entwined. It's easy with him now, which I never thought it would be. Almost losing the love of your life does that. It makes you see things in a different light, encourages you to quit setting the small shit and forces you to appreciate the little moments. Our little moments are my favorite.

"I have to grab something I made for the baby." He carefully puts the tires of the truck into the ruts that have been made.

"When are you guys going to get some blacktop out here? It's crazy how much time all y'all spend out here, but you don't fix the road."

He lets go of my hand, shoving the truck into four-wheel-drive and grins as he guns it, to get over a mountain of mud. "Maybe we like to drive it without blacktop."

He's got this grin. It's what I call his little boy grin. Before eight months ago, I'd never seen it. Never would've dreamed he would be so carefree, but this man of mine – he's learned to enjoy life. Maybe I've had a little bit of an influence on him, and Darren? He's had an even bigger influence on him.

We learned two days ago we'll be able to officially adopt him at the beginning of the year. As a family, we are more excited than we can explain. We're planning on purchasing a house and giving Darren the life he should have been living all along. As soon as those papers go through, his last name will be Kepler. Even though mine won't be, I'll still be listed as his mother, and that's okay with me.

"Here we go," he announces as we pull up to the shop. "Wanna get out with me?"

"You mean I'm allowed to go into your mancave?" I tease him, giggling when he makes a face. Glancing up at the sky, I see clouds rolling in. "Looks like it's gonna rain."

"We should be out of here before the rain rolls in." He grabs my hand, leading me to the entrance.

There's something sexy about watching the man who loves me, do things with authority, and damned if he doesn't unlock this door with authority. "After you." He motions.

When I go in, I'm assaulted with the scent of fresh pine and the lacquer he puts on some pieces. In the corner, there's a shelf of handmade wooden toys. "These are beautiful."

"They're for the big Christmas drive we're having this year. I made one for every kid with an angel on the tree." He shuffles his feet.

"God, I love you." I cross the room, putting my arms around him. "You have such a great heart."

"Only because you allowed me to find it." He leans down, kissing me softly on the lips.

Walking across the shop, he grabs a wooden sign. "If I show you this, I'll have to kill you." He jokes. "It's got the baby's name on it."

"Are you kidding me? You know the sex?" Ransom and Stella found out, but they refuse to tell anyone else.

"Unfortunately no, they picked a fuckin' unisex name. Keegan N. Thompson."

"Assholes," I hiss. "Could be Nickolas or Nicole."

"Exactly, they suck," he agrees. "C'mon, let's get this stuff into the truck and we can be on our way. I'll drop this off to them when we go pick up Darren."

"Sounds good to me."

We walk outside as the first drops begin to fall. He goes to the covered bed, storing the wooden sign there, to keep it from getting wet. "Nick, open the door!" I yell as I try the passenger side but it's locked up tight.

He doesn't hear, and I can't see him around the back. "Nick," I try again.

That's when the covered bed closes and he walks toward me. "You can just click the locks."

He smiles, the slightly crooked, sexy smile that he does for me and me alone now. "No I can't just click the locks."

"Why not?" I swallow roughly as he gets to where I am.

We're standing in the rain, buckets pouring over us as we stare at one another. His hand goes to my cheek, threading his fingers through my hair. "Because, I remember you saying something to me once about the rain."

I wrack my brain, trying to remember what I said. It hits me like a ton of bricks. He must notice a change in my face, because he nods his head slowly before dropping to a knee.

"You told me once that you thought the perfect proposal

would be in the rain." Both of us are shaking as he takes hold of my hand. "I've been thinking about it a lot lately – what my life is like now, how you've made such positive changes in it, how you helped me when I got shot, and most of all how you love me, and in turn allow me to love you."

"Nick," I whisper.

"So I planned this, hoping the weather would cooperate." He looks up the sky. "And it did. I know how important it is to you have thought-out gifts, and I want you to know I've worked on this and thought about it a lot over the past few months. Kelsea Harrison, will you marry me?"

My heart is pounding against my chest, and I fear I'll hyperventilate. All of a sudden, I realize I'm just staring at him like an idiot. "Yes! Yes! Yes!" I answer.

It's then I notice he's holding a wooden box in his hand. "Did you make this?"

"I did," he confirms as he gives it to me.

Rolling it around in my fingers, I see he's carved little parts of our life together on there. There are little symbols of what's come to be our love. The way we like to cook together, watch TV with Darren, and the quiet nights we like to spend as a family. There are flowers, which is what I love to do, and I see an American flag with a thin blue line on it, his interest being represented. "Can I open it?"

"It's yours, babe. It and my heart are yours, Kelsea. I love you so deeply, so damn strongly, some days I don't know what to do with myself."

"The feeling is mutual, I love you too." I bend down, kissing him softly against his lips.

With shaking hands of my own, I open the box, gasping when I see a sapphire and diamond ring twinkling back at me. "It was my grandmother's," he says softly. "She gave it to me not long ago, saying she was happy when I came into the family because she would have someone to pass it down to. Tank and Blaze aren't sticklers for history, but you Kels, you know what this shit means."

"They were married for sixty years before your grandpa died." I cry harder. "This ring knew a lot of love."

"It did, babe, and it'll know a lifetime more."

"I'll pass it on to Darren." I wipe at my eyes. "Put it on me, please."

He slides it quickly onto my finger. It fits perfectly.

"We're going to have an amazing life, Kels. I promise. I love you so much it scares the fuck outta me."

Throwing my arms around his waist, I bury my head in his chest, letting the rain wash my tears away. "I believe you, Nick. I've always believed you. I love you too."

With those words, he picks me up, spinning me around, both of us laughing. For a girl whose had some pretty amazing moments in her life – this one? It's completely perfect.

EPILOGUE TWO

Kelsea

"C'mon you two, we're running late," I yell through the apartment as I throw open the closet door, looking for my flats. If we need to run to make it on time, at least I'll have proper footwear.

"Dad, I don't know how to tie my tie!"

It still gets me, hearing him call us Mom and Dad, today, all of that becomes official.

"Be there in just a second," Nick yells back as he stands up from the bed, tucking his button-down into his slacks. "I can't believe we overslept."

"It's not our fault the power went out, and it knocked out the cell phone service too," I grab a tube of gloss, putting it on my lips as I run a brush through my hair.

"Okay, so for the tie," Nick looks at Darren. "That's something we'll get your grandpa to do, D-man, I still can't tie my own tie."

The quiet in the room is deafening before we all bust out in nervous laughter. "Let's go," I point towards the door. "Everyone's gonna meet us there."

We're quiet as we make our way to the Laurel Springs courthouse. All of us lost in our own thoughts about what today means. As we approach, I see the fleet of vehicles that's shown up for us.

"Who is all of that?" Darren asks from the backseat.

Nick turns, a boyish grin on his face. "That's your family, D. That's our family."

I'm overcome with emotion as I see everyone who means the world to us. Parents, friends, other family. Karsyn is there, hanging back from Tucker, but knowing they aren't really speaking to one another right now, I'm so thankful that they both showed up.

Nick parks, before we all hop out.

"We need tie help," Darren yells immediately.

"That's all on you," my dad looks to Ryan. "I've never been able to do it."

Ryan kneels with emotion on his face. I don't hear what they say, but I take a picture with my phone because I want this memory to last forever, even as it fades. He hugs Darren, then stands up to help Nick. They joke and laugh as they get the job done.

This side of Nick I've seen in the last few months, is one I never thought I'd see. He smiles, he laughs, he makes jokes. The two of us grin at one another as the whole group starts walking towards the courthouse.

Today is going to be the day that we become a family.

Nick

I don't think I've ever been so nervous in my life, except maybe when I proposed to Kels. We got married a week ago, eloped right here at the courthouse so that we could all have the same last name. That's gonna be a surprise for everyone too. Ransom, Stelle, and D-man were our witnesses.

When we walk into the courtroom, we're greeted with decorations and a cake congratulating us on becoming a family. I'm hit with emotion I haven't felt since I was adopted.

"You ready?" I grip Darren's shoulders as he stands in front of me.

"I've never been so ready."

To be honest, I don't hear most of what's being said, the only thing I hear are the words that matter.

"Darren Metcalfe, do you agree to the adoption, and your name changing to Darren Kepler?"

"Yes!" He screams so loudly it causes a flurry of noise.

We're called to the front, to sign our names. "Congratulations to Nickolas, Kelsea, and Darren Kepler, you're now a family."

"Her last name is Harrison," Caleb coughs.

We grin at one another. "No it's not," she shakes her head. "We got married last week."

The noise is deafening, and there's someone trying to get our picture.

"Can I get one of the family?"

"If you want one of the family, you'll have to fit us all in," I tell him loudly. "C'mon y'all!"

One by one I see them walk up. Ransom, Cutter, Stella, Rambo, Leigh, Havoc, Mom, Dad, Ace, Violet, Tank, Blaze, Caleb, Ruby, Molly, Levi, Menace, Karina, Tucker, Karsyn, Dr. Patterson, everyone who means anything to us is here.

"Okay, say family."

I grab the hand of my wife, put my own hand on the shoulder of my son, and say the word that's gotten me from where I was to where I am today. "Family!"

The End

THANK YOU!

Thank you so much for reading "Suppression"! If this was your first book mine, I would love it if you would look the others up. The Heaven Hill Series and Moonshine Task Force are reader favorites!

If there was a part you loved of "Suppression", please don't hesitate to leave a review and let other readers know!

Also, if you do leave a review, please email me with the link so that I can say a personal 'thank you'!!! They mean a lot, and I want to let you know I appreciate you taking the time out of your day!

Email Me

Also, if you find an error, know that it has slipped through no less than four sets of eyes, and it is a mistake. Please let me know, if you find one, and if I agree it's an error. It will be changed. Thank you!

Report an error

CONNECT

Connect with Laramie:

Website: http://www.laramiebriscoe.net

Facebook: https://www.facebook.com/AuthorLaramieBriscoe

Twitter: https://twitter.com/LaramieBriscoe

Pinterest: http://www.pinterest.com/laramiebriscoe/

Instagram: http://instagram.com/laramie_briscoe

Mailing List: sitel.ink/LBList

Email: Laramie@laramiebriscoe.com

Made in the USA
Las Vegas, NV
18 January 2021